Life Unbothered

Charlie Elliott

Published by Waldorf Publishing
2140 Hall Johnson Road
#102-345
Grapevine, Texas 76051
www.WaldorfPublishing.com

Life Unbothered

ISBN: 978-1-945175-28-2
Library of Congress Control Number: 2016957022

Copyright © 2017

All rights reserved. No part of this book may be reproduced or transmitted in any form or by any means whatsoever without express written permission from the author, except in the case of brief quotations embodied in critical articles and reviews. Please refer all pertinent questions to the publisher. All rights reserved. No part of this book may be reproduced or transmitted in any form or by any means, electronic or mechanical, including photocopying, recording, or by an information storage and retrieval system except by a reviewer who may quote brief passages in a review to be printed in a magazine or newspaper without permission in writing from the publisher.

For those with resolve.

CONTENTS

1. A Fine Arizona Morning…1
2. The Morning After…9
3. The Neighbor…17
4. The Shortest Distance Between Two Points…24
5. More Doctors…38
6. The Intervention…50
7. Puddle Jump…59
8. The Tightrope…71
9. The Return…83
10. It's About the Sex…95
11. For Something a Little Different…109
12. Golfing with the Enemy…115
13. The Slumber Party…126
14. Employment…135
15. The Encounter…142
16. The Kiss…149
17. The Love…162
18. The Apron…175
19. The Pact…188
20. The Canyon…196
21. Taking Care…208
22. The Fall…215
23. Fashionably Late…219
24. The Diagnosis…235
25. The Change…242
26. The Eve…248
27. Come to the Parade…259
28. Swallow…264
29. Expiration…268
30. Getting Air…274

About The Author…282

1. A Fine Arizona Morning

What should have been a desolate drive had turned out to be a postcard-perfect April morning. The sun peered over the McDowell Mountains to the east, not yet ready to lift the cool blue shadows shrouding the inert desert paradise. Immersed in the landscape of shifting pastels and crisp, sage-scented air, I was periodically forced to remind myself of what I was looking for. I was looking for a place to kill myself.

My BMW glided along a straight undulating road at eighty miles per hour, creating a roller-coaster effect as I headed north of Scottsdale, away from the greater Phoenix urban area. The intermittent sound of pebbles pelting the wheel wells began when I slowed the car and made a random turn down an unnamed, unpaved road.

"Wade, where are we going?" Pamela Wains, my fiancée, asked in an annoying high-pitched tone.

"I'm going to hell," I muttered.

"Wade, that's not funny. Don't be an asshole. We're getting married in two weeks."

I started hyperventilating and pursed my lips to absorb the apprehension. I looked up nervously at the clear sky through my windshield and pondered events that brought me to this state. The insistent gravity of my thoughts seemed to press me deeper into the car seat.

"So where are we going?" Pamela asked again.

"I'm not quite sure. I'm looking for a place."

"We're out in the middle of nowhere," Pamela noted. "Are you taking me shopping or something?"

"No shopping. Just looking for a place to rest."

"Are we going to a restaurant?"

I exhaled and closed my eyes for a couple of seconds. "Pamela, do you see anything remotely resembling a restaurant out here? You're the one who insisted on going with me. I didn't even want you to come along."

"I just want to know where the hell we're going," Pamela screeched.

In an attempt to end the conversation immediately, I grasped both hands on the steering wheel and yanked it hard to the right. The car skidded sideways on the dry dirt until it left the road entirely and proceeded to execute a one-hundred-eighty-degree slide. The tail end whipped around and clipped a large saguaro cactus. Still almost thirty miles outside of Scottsdale, the prickly giant was safe for at least a decade from the ever-encroaching metropolitan area. Unfortunately, the cactus still had to contend with crazed drivers and their personal problems.

Dust engulfed me when I swung the door open and exited the car. As I perused the landscape through the floating haze, a mini-forest of mesquite trees rose above the outcroppings of brittlebush. A dotting of saguaro cacti stood proudly with upturned arms as if giving a greeting wave, welcoming me to my death place. I went to the back of the car to discover an eight-inch-deep gash in the cactus I hit during the uncontrolled turn. The bushwhacked green giant remained standing proud and still, seemingly content despite the fact my bumper had almost obliterated sixty years of undisturbed growth. My car appeared undamaged, but I didn't care to check it thoroughly.

I crossed my arms and bowed my head after I scanned the scenery. I suddenly felt insecure, out in the open, self-conscious. Pamela bounded out of the car as I stared at a cluster of round pebbles dotting the sandy desert soil.

"Wade, you almost killed me, you idiot," she said. "What the hell is wrong with you?"

Without responding, I opened the trunk to retrieve my loaded Beretta nine-millimeter pistol. Placing the gun in there the night before was the only prior planning I had done for the morning drive. I was too lazy to write a suicide note or even pay the current bills. My incomplete last will would take care of all the pesky details.

The gun sat against the side of the trunk wedged behind the hose that delivered fuel to the gas tank. After freeing the weapon, I inspected the magazine. All ten rounds were intact, but I knew I only needed one, or possibly two if my aim was askew. I cast a stern look in Pamela's direction, absently noting the ample makeup applied around her eyes gave her the look of a raccoon wearing false lashes.

"You're shittin' me," she said. "You took me out here to shoot your gun? I hate guns. If you're not taking me somewhere I can enjoy, you're just wasting my time, Wade."

I started walking away from my car, not sure which way to go. I was scouting for a place… an appropriate locale to do it. I walked through the low-lying desert scrub, leaving behind the narrow dirt road that had delivered us to this empty place. Out of the brush, a desert rat scurried across my path to safety. I had invaded its space, but planned to be a neighbor soon.

I was astounded that Pamela actually followed me in silence while I walked with a gun in my hand. With every step, the friction created by her painted-on jeans made a faint whistling sound as her thighs rubbed together. The black plastic tassels strewn across her burnt orange shirt jostled from side to side casting irritating little tink tink noises that progressed with her strides. Her designer boots scraped patches of hardpan as she trailed a couple of steps behind.

I stopped walking as a warm, gentle breeze flowed around me and adrenaline clogged my ear canals. A couple of roadrunners bustled in the sagebrush a few feet off, but the beauty of the arid natural surroundings escaped me. What troubled me most was the uncertainty of not knowing whether my cerebral havoc would ever cease, and how I had come to be an embarrassment to myself and felt others around me shared the same viewpoint. Now that the decision was made to end it all, my family would no longer need to explain what I'm doing, where I'm working, or what woman I'm shacking up with. Pamela Wains could justify her canceled wedding.

With my back turned to her, I said, "Pamela, I'm going to kill myself."

"You're going to kill yourself now? Two weeks before our wedding?"

I turned to her and dropped my arm, letting the gun rest by my hip. "Pamela, is that your biggest concern at the moment? I don't want to get married, I want to die. Can you comprehend that?"

"You don't want to get married?" Pamela's voice hit an uncharted octave. "Seriously!" She kicked the dirt with her fancy boot and spun an angry circle before facing me again. Sudden tears cut black gutters through her thickly applied mascara. "Fuck you. We could've gotten married first and then you could kill yourself if you weren't happy." She puffed out a forced breath. "I can't believe you."

"Pamela, you want to be married to a guy who's standing with a gun out in the middle of the desert about to off himself?"

She kicked some more desert dirt around and creased her dark brown eyebrows. "That's it! This is the last time I get involved with some spoiled psycho idiot. You've taken some of the best months of my life, Wade. I'm no longer going to be nice—so go ahead and do it. I'll keep your car after you're done here," she paused and scanned the empty land that rolled out for miles, "wherever the shitstink we are."

Fighting a sudden urge to aim at Pamela and pull the trigger, I decided to spare her and get to the original business at hand. As I lifted the matte-black gun to the side of my head, I felt the hard mouth of the barrel press against my hair.

A crackling crossfire of troubles wracked my mind as I tried to validate my decision. I started to think not of whom my suicide might affect and the pernicious repercussions, but about how I would look, all stupid and everything, dead in the middle of the desert. It would be embarrassing, all those strangers gawking at my debrided neck and head. And my clothes—wrinkled and soiled. I would come off as an idiot.

I heard a faint shriek come from Pamela as she tried to reinforce her new tough self. "Go ahead Wade, just get your pathetic life over with." She kicked the ground again. "'Don't want to get married.' Shit."

Although I was able to ignore the hard-wired trepidation that comes along with contemplating the most unnatural act a sentient being can commit, I felt a little offended by Pamela's half-hearted objections. The plan had played out so much easier in my mental skit the night before, but I hadn't expected her to come along for the ride. Suicide was supposed to be a solo sport.

I pulled the gun away from my scalp and felt a breeze soothe the now-sweaty circle where the end of the barrel had been. The cartoonish image of methodically working my way up my body before blowing my head off came to mind. *Inch into the cold pool, don't dive*. I pointed the gun at my left knee and winced.

Pamela belted out a nervous laugh. "Oh, that's great, you're going to shoot your knee now. That's smart, Wade."

I looked up at Pamela from my awkward stance in sudden embarrassment. I couldn't even kill myself the right way.

"Just forget it," I said. I pulled the gun away from my knee and straightened my posture. I cocked my right arm and heaved the gun. It twisted round and round through the air for about fifty feet until there was a brief muffled sound of crunching twigs—BANG! The gun discharged as it hit the ground, sending a bullet somewhere into the sky. Startled, I jumped about a foot into the air. Pamela's fake blonde bangs jabbed her widened eyeballs as she looked skyward, her head turned as if she'd traced the bullet's path.

"You're nuts," Pamela shouted in disbelief.

Having no interest in retrieving the gun, I started walking in the direction of my car, blindly backtracking the same pathless route. Pamela just stood in place, refusing to join me.

I looked back at her while still walking. "Are you coming?"

"You're fucking nuts. I wouldn't go anywhere with you."

I stopped for a moment. "You mean... you want me to leave you out here?"

"I'm not going anywhere with you, you sick bastard." Her shrill voice echoed to the hills.

I shrugged my shoulders and continued back to the road.

When I got to my car, I hesitated before opening the door and saw Pamela standing a couple hundred feet away and not moving any closer to the car. She was standing her ground and feverishly fingering her cell phone, probably letting the texts fly. *I am a sick bastard*, I mumbled as I got in the car to begin the drive home. Alone.

2. The Morning After

"Wake up, Jerk," I heard from above.

My left eyelid parted slightly, letting a crack of brightness flare into my eye. By the position of the sunlight in the room and the stiffness in my outstretched legs, I was suddenly aware that I had been asleep on the living room couch from the time I got home after the botched suicide attempt and had slept through the entire night. I opened my right eye and blinked once to adjust my focus and wash away the filmy cover impeding my sight. My refreshed vision revealed Pamela Wains hovering over me, her head silhouetted by the morning sun. Her ten-shades-lighter-than-natural blonde hair flopped over her eyes, partially concealing the indignation they held. I noticed the thick purple terrycloth robe she wore added some weight to her wiry body.

"How'd you get home?"

"I called a friend. I had to walk about three miles for her to find me. Luckily there was cell service. You owe me some dry cleaning and a new pair of boots."

"Where did you spend the night?" I asked, not out of curiosity, the question just came out of my mouth as I was still coming to a fully awakened state.

"What the fuck do you care? I'm moving out. I found an apartment."

"Where?"

"In Tempe."

I rolled my eyes while sitting up on the couch. "Pamela, are you really moving this time?"

"I'm not shitting you, I'm moving. You don't want to get married, and… you're crazy. Geez, you almost killed yourself yesterday. I can forget that and we can go on, but you said you don't want to get married."

"Remember the last time you said you were leaving?" I asked.

"You bought me that necklace when I came back." She tightened her face. "It'll take a lot more this time."

"Pamela, there is no gift this time."

"Nothing for me?"

"No, sorry."

"Well then, I'm really going," she said with a manufactured smile.

"Who's going to move you?"

"The movers at the apartment complex. They're coming around noon."

I looked at my watch. "Noon?"

"I can cancel it," she said, then shifted her mouth to one side and bit her lower lip. "But you'll have to pay the lost deposit and tell me you still want to get married."

"Pamela, I don't have any gifts for you this time. And no, I can't go on like this."

Pamela and I locked into a staredown. Her beaming eyes packed such fury that it felt like rays were shooting through my eyes and into my brain, making the back of my already aching head puddle with warmth. She finally broke her gaze and strutted a few stompy steps to the landline phone perched upon the lone end table in the room.

She plucked the wireless receiver off its base while I remained seated motionless on the couch. With her lips pursed and face scrunched tight, she turned back to face me and lifted her right foot as if taking an abnormally high step. Focusing on her leg movement, I failed to see her right arm winding back with the receiver. Pamela's body lunged forward, releasing the receiver from her hand. My reflexes didn't allow me to flinch fast enough as the unit smacked my left cheek squarely before making a bouncy landing on the couch cushion. I wrenched my hand to my cheek as the cracking sound of plastic striking bone radiated down my neck. The front of my head instantaneously acquired the same balmy pain as the back. Pamela glared at me and crossed her arms. Her robe's tattered sleeves dangled little purple hairs that grabbed her forearms. She huffed once and strutted into the master bedroom. The sound of flying objects started rippling through the house.

"Pamela, come on," I said.

Her face was bright red when she re-entered the living room. "I'm moving! Leave me alone while I pack some stuff."

I had become quite good at dodging items Pamela threw at me occasionally, but with the phone, her proximity was too close for me to avoid. I rose hesitantly from the couch and fetched an ice cube from the refrigerator to soothe the throbbing left side of my phone-struck face. As Pamela stormed the house with a pinched look on her face, I tended to a stack of newly washed underwear and placed them on the ironing board situated in the small dining room between the kitchen and living room. I meticulously pressed a pair of my boxer shorts with the iron in my right hand while the ice cube in my left hand worked my cheek. I remained at the ironing board taking wrinkles out of all my underwear. Then I went to work on a clump of socks.

With every new drip of ice water down my cheek, anxiety sprang from my stomach, taking its familiar passage to my extremities. It was two weeks before the wedding was supposed to occur, but I couldn't believe that I let the whole relationship get to any point remotely resembling marriage.

To me, Pamela's presence was merely Spackle to fill the cracks of my vacant soul. I wish I could tell her it was just the tangible presence of women I loved, that crutch keeping me from locking myself into a room, that sexual babysitter who comforts me with a blanket of contact and release. It would be nice if I had the guts to tell her that I had fooled around with other women since our first date. I wish I told her earlier in the relationship to go and marry one of the managers at her bank job and have a nice uncomplicated life. I could never divulge to her the fact that my own brain had failed her because a disease with no physical symptoms influenced my decisions, and the engagement ring I presented to her six months before was an emotional mistake that for a fleeting moment trumped my personal reservations. Pamela showed up at my house a few days after the engagement with all her possessions and thirty thousand dollars worth of high-interest credit card debt. Blindsided and weakened by mental fatigue, I let her stay.

Once moved in, she would spend her evenings watching some TV drama coupled with an endless array of manicures, pedicures, mud masks, hair treatments, cellophane fat wraps, hair removal gadgets and eyebrow plucks while simultaneously chatting with her friends on the phone. Bedtime progressed into a period of affectionless sleep. Pamela viewed the act of sex as a necessary evil—merely a dirty little component that goes along with a relationship. I knew my mind wouldn't let it succeed. From the beginning, wedded failure was a given.

As Pamela scurried around the house sorting clothes and tagging furniture to take, I learned she was moving to Palm Courtyard, a new two-story apartment complex at the south end of Tempe, close to the neighboring city of Mesa. The brochure from the complex presented a typical white stucco development that seemed to be popping up weekly in the greater Phoenix area. Palm Courtyard was about twenty miles away from my house in Scottsdale, and close to where Pamela used to live when we met. The new complex offered to move people locally free of charge.

Pamela stuffed smaller items into her Toyota with assistance from her friend, Tammy, who arrived shortly after I had finished all of my ironing. Tammy always struck me as cute, but immature. She was a twenty-four-year-old non-prescription medicine salesperson whose unwavering bubbly personality was stuck in high school cheerleader mode. The two pecked around the house nervously in search of things to snatch. I tried to remain casual as I stalked after them, as if I weren't watching what they were taking, but they were keenly aware I was.

Emotions sparked when Pamela took one last romp through the wedding presents. Though all the gifts we received were from people invited by my side of the family, practically every gift she had registered for arrived magically at our doorstep. Pamela eyed the partially opened box of Lenox Grand Affair china stacked among the other gifts. The box contained twelve complete place settings. It was an artfully understated, classy set accented in platinum. She grabbed one of the plates and hugged the inanimate object like a beloved kitten.

"It's so pretty, I want to keep it," Pamela cried.

She also wanted the eight Baccarat vases that arrived a few weeks earlier. They were apparently expensive, but I had questioned what the hell we were going to do with eight crystal vases.

"I want these too," she said as saliva shot out of her mouth and landed on one of the vases.

"No, I'm going to have to return all the gifts," I said.

Tammy watched Pamela snivel over the gifts and threw dirty looks my way, bolstering my belief that in her eyes I could qualify as a finalist in the Biggest Asshole of the Universe competition.

A few minutes before noon, two men arrived in an unmarked white cube van to lug the stuff away. It took the complimentary movers just under an hour to load all the larger items before vanishing down the road.

Tammy scurried through the front door to flee the scene as Pamela performed her last walkthrough around the house, idly snatching a few remaining knick-knacks for her new abode. The last item she grabbed was a square red ceramic dish signed by a purportedly famous hippie artist from Sedona. It was actually my dish, but in the moment it was her right to relinquish it from my possessions.

"I just wanted to tell you," she turned to me while still clutching the hippie dish and said as if rehearsed, "this is the shittiest thing anyone has ever done to me."

Pamela's thickly applied mascara began sponging up some of the tears falling from her brown eyes. I extended my arm to attempt a gentle shoulder rub. The gesture was more of a reflex than an act of tenderness.

"You're better off without me," I said.

"Oh, screw you, Wade. Screw you!" she shouted, and then pulled a step away from me. "I have to go now."

She exited the house with my signed red dish in her hand. The departure should have been a somber occasion, but the burden of cohabitation and impending matrimony lifted off me immediately after she slammed the front door. I wanted to go and refold my clothes she threw on the floor while whirling about the house, but hesitated for a minute to let some internal relief seep into my skin. My conscious struggled with the contrasting feelings of remorse coupled with elation. It was sad that my relief came at the painful expense of someone else. But relief won out, it was my survival mechanism.

3. The Neighbor

With Pamela gone and the wedding off, I knew I should make some calls and alert people about the change of plans—especially my parents. Instead, I opted to procrastinate. So I went outside and mowed the small patch of Bermuda lawn in the backyard, then took the wet/dry shop vacuum to the rock garden that covered the entire front yard.

Due to the desert climate, many homes in the Phoenix area had a layer of small rocks covering their yards instead of a lush lawn. Rocks did not require watering or mowing, nor did they turn brown in the winter, freeze, or dry up. They were just there—consistent all the time, never changing. I liked the rock front yard; it was efficient and low maintenance. The yard mirrored my ideal relationship—though humans were much more complicated than decorative pebbles.

After attempting to rake the leaves deposited mainly from an olive and a eucalyptus tree in the front yard, the inch-long white craggy rocks would also rake up into a big pile. I had yet to discover a leaf and rock-straining device, so using the six-horsepower vacuum to suck the leaves off the top of the rocks made sense. The vacuum used to clean the interiors of fine European cars at my auto detailing shop. Since the closing of the business a couple of months before, its demoted function consisted of outdoor leaf duty.

As I was stretching the extension cord far enough for the vacuum to reach the rocks by the driveway, a sensual throaty voice came from behind me.

"You're not only the sexiest man I know, you're also the smartest."

I smiled and turned around. "Hi Colleen."

"You know, that yard-vacuuming process is ingenious. Why doesn't anyone else do that?"

"I don't know. It could be some people don't have one of these vacuums sitting around the house—and a thousand feet worth of extension cords."

Colleen was a forty-nine-year-old divorcee who moved next door about two months after I engaged Pamela. Besides having a figure that put many younger women to shame, she was a very attractive brunette with large natural breasts that were surprisingly unshakeable.

Colleen had a habit of inviting me over on nights when coincidently, Pamela would be out for "girls' night," an event that occurred about twice a month. I never figured out how Colleen knew Pamela's social schedule, but she would ceremoniously ring my doorbell shortly after Pamela's departure.

Colleen would grace my doorstep with some problem she thought I could fix—dripping faucet, toilet leak, or a chore that required standing on a ladder. When free of handyman tasks, she would simply ask me to share a home-cooked meal. Colleen was intelligent, educated, and had traveled extensively with her pediatrician ex-husband who she caught one afternoon with a nurse two decades younger than her.

As Colleen tiptoed over the freshly vacuumed rocks to move closer, I admired her curvaceous body. The white sundress she wore complemented her dark brown hair and lightly tanned skin.

"I saw Pamela skid out of the driveway earlier," she said.

"Yeah, I know. I broke off the wedding. She found an apartment and moved out."

Colleen lifted her eyebrows. "Oh really? And here I thought she was just being her usual cheerful self."

I laughed. "Probably so."

With delicate care, she brushed the left side of my face with two fingers. "Your cheek looks a little red."

"Pamela threw a phone at me."

"Ouch. I take it she's not pleased with you."

"You could say that."

"Don't get me wrong. I'm sorry about the wedding, but I don't see how you could've been happy with her."

"I know, but it still doesn't make it any easier."

Colleen glanced in the direction of my zipper and then gradually lifted her eyes to meet mine.

"Come on over for some lemonade," she said. "You can finish your vacuuming later."

I lifted my arm to wipe my brow. "I'm kind of sweaty from all the yard work."

"That's okay. You never minded my sweat." She turned around and started walking slowly, giving me a view of her shapely backside as a dry, gentle breeze ruffled her dress.

"Yeah, you always taste good," I mumbled as I dropped the vacuum hose and obediently followed her next door.

I perched myself on a wrought iron barstool in Colleen's kitchen. She stood opposite me on the other side of the counter and poured two glasses of fresh-squeezed lemonade.

"Wade, don't knock yourself down about this. Everything will work out for the better."

I took a sip of lemonade. The tart taste surprised my palate and awakened me from the drone of merely doing yard work to sitting in the house of a very desirable woman discussing my botched relationship that happened right next door in our quiet, unassuming neighborhood.

"Not getting married to Pamela is a big relief. Just my parents and friends… everyone went through a lot of work for me to back out of the wedding—not to mention the money. That's what really gets me."

Colleen mustered a cute little grin. "I remember you saying something about the costs. I thought tradition, not that it means much anymore, calls for the bride's family to cover the costs. Why exactly were your parents paying for the whole wedding?"

"Well…" I struggled to find the most accurate wording as my thumb rubbed against the chilled glass. "When Pamela and I became engaged, she said she wanted a fairytale wedding. You know, all the stuff that girls dream about on their 'most important day'. The problem was Pamela's dad got laid off about a month before our engagement."

"Where did he work?"

"He was vice president of passenger side seatbelt clasps at one of the automakers."

"Vice president for passenger seatbelt… clasps," Colleen said with a suppressed laugh. "They have an actual VP for that?"

"Auto companies have thousands of vice presidents, even for that. Those guys are mainly just functionaries. But I feel for him. A downward tick in revenue resulted in huge layoffs. After thirty years there, he got the boot."

"Her dad probably became worried when you got engaged."

"Oh, he did. Her parents got into immediate financial trouble after the layoff. Pamela's wedding wishes freaked them out. I told my dad about it one night and he said it would be no problem to give Pamela a wedding fit for a queen. The only stipulation was we would get married in Los Angeles instead of her hometown of Detroit."

"How did she take that?"

"Are you kidding? When I told her, she was ecstatic. Pamela didn't care where the wedding was, just so it was the most extravagant event she could imagine."

Colleen leaned over the counter. "You know, she's not the brightest tube in a row of fluorescent lights."

I sighed and drank another sip of lemonade. "Yeah, I realize that. But I just thought at age twenty-seven it was time for me to get married."

I put my elbows on the counter and leaned forward. Colleen lowered her head and pecked me on the lips.

"Age doesn't matter. You're still a young pup." She paused for a moment and slowly ran her finger around the top of her glass. "Anyway, if Pamela is such a great catch, why do we fool around?"

A wry grin plastered across my face. "Because you're an alluring older woman taking advantage of a young impressionable pup."

"And you're one of the biggest charmers I've ever met," she said. We leaned closer again and enjoyed an extended kiss.

After pulling away, Colleen walked around the counter and stood in front of me. "God, I bet Pamela is going to miss the sex."

"Pamela doesn't even like sex."

"That's too bad. Your notable talents shouldn't go to waste."

"My so-called talents get me in trouble sometimes."

"No, your trouble probably intensified when you let that girl move in." Colleen bit her lower lip playfully and clasped her hands on both sides of her sundress, gradually lifting it to just beneath her breasts. "No more wedding talk for now."

I gazed at her bare bottom half while a sultry comfort flowed within me. Colleen lowered herself to the carpeted floor and I stretched my neck as I flopped down to join her. My lips kissed her right knee before traveling up to the top of her opening legs. When my tongue parted her, wedding blues dissipated as I became absorbed in Colleen's welcoming femininity.

4. The Shortest Distance Between Two Points

There's an inherent flaw with thinking the world is one big joke. Through my somewhat charmed youth, I believed life was set in place and there was no urgent reason to sweat any of the little details—with scant effort it was all supposed to work out in grand fashion. As my age kept going up the scale, the world had somehow shifted its orbit, and the joke was now on me. With canceled nuptials, as with most planned events that suddenly don't exist, some loose ends needed attending to. I contemplated going back over to Colleen's house for another glass of lemonade, but I found calling off a wedding one of those anti-joke worldly events that couldn't afford any further time to linger. I wrote a letter to all invited guests from my side informing them there had been an unfortunate turn in my impending wedding to Pamela and we had decided to call off the ceremony indefinitely. The letter was short, about a half page, typewritten on my laptop. It had the tone of a corporate memo and lacked any discernible emotion. It fit my state of mind. Sending them by old-fashioned postal mail conveyed formality of finality, plus it gave me a couple of days of cushion to brace for the questions that would undoubtedly follow from the receivers. I emailed Richard, my best man, to let him know the wedding was off but not to tell anyone until I informed my parents.

After taking a quick inventory to verify none of the gratuities had disappeared when Pamela moved, I repacked all the wedding presents. It took five separate trips to the local shipping store to return the boxes back to their donors. I could just picture the hassle I had created by not getting married and the dismay of my guests having to return their gifts to an array department stores, boutiques, or online merchants.

When I finished shipping the gifts, I went to the kitchen counter and looked at the next task on my to-do list: Move the remaining furniture around. From the third bedroom, I carried the BarcaLounger recliner into the living room. To complement the new living room décor, I also moved an old computer printer stand and the forty-inch flat screen TV from the rarely used bedroom and set them up against the bare white wall. I then walked into the other small guest bedroom and lifted the queen-sized mattress off its box springs. Propping the mattress on its side, I dragged it through the narrow hallway to replace the now absent king in the master bedroom.

Pamela and her movers managed to take all the master bedroom furniture, most of the portable kitchen appliances, the living room and dining room sets, the larger of the two televisions, and the narrow front entry table. None of the furniture was actually hers, but I let it all go, sparing an argument over replaceable material possessions. I was relieved she didn't find my iron, which I had tucked away in the garage while her attention was focused on other household items. Luckily, she also passed on the ironing board, but she did regard it for a moment before a framed lithograph on the laundry room wall caught her eye.

I scanned the open living area and saw how stark it was now that Pamela had removed most of the visible items. The house, though the same on the outside, was transformed into a minimalist's dream on the inside. It was a three bedroom, one story light brown brick and cinder block house in a middle-class section located in the north end of Scottsdale. Its sixteen-hundred square-foot bare interior lacked any sense of a functional family home; the dwelling now resembled that of a misled bachelor who refused to grow up.

The emptiness intensified the fact that it was time to start a new chapter in my life. With no healing process in mind, I decided to do as I had in the past—disappear from my current surroundings. I finished setting up the bed in the master bedroom and walked into my closet. The built-in shelves now accommodated my boxers, t-shirts and shorts Pamela had hurled from the dresser before the movers arrived. After I had re-ironed all the clothes, I stowed them in the closet. Without any deep effort to conforming color schemes or matching outfits, I placed a few days' worth of clothing into a travel bag. Then I went into the bathroom to fetch some essential toiletries and my compact travel iron.

The destination would be my hometown of Palos Verdes, a well-heeled suburb on the southern coast of Los Angeles, to tell my parents in person that the wedding they were paying for wasn't going to be.

The four hundred mile journey began at half past five. After winding through the expansive Phoenix area for twenty minutes, my car merged on to Interstate 10. I was a bit ahead of the setting sun, knowing the bright orange ball would eventually greet my face for about an hour before outracing my car and disappearing into the westward horizon.

Ten miles outside the furthest stretches of Phoenix, the population abated and exposed land folded out in front of me. I knew what was coming. The openness of the land and sky was a problem. Being in an enclosed space was a problem. The combination would automatically trigger the emotion center in my brain to make sure I knew that danger was present. And if the initial rippling wasn't enough to evoke a response, my mind would overcompensate to ensure I got the message. The city was gone, the access to doctors was gone, my house was becoming farther away. All factors were testing my sanity.

In the middle of nowhere.

The sinister sentence popped into my head repeatedly. There was no interesting scenery to gaze at to help diffuse the anxiety, just thin green mile marker signs whizzing by every forty-five seconds. Attempting to shrug off the chant, I continued to speed into the vast unpopulated desert, creeping away from the security of the Phoenix metropolitan area.

In the middle of nowhere. In the middle of nowhere.

I passed Tonopah, a little town forty miles west of downtown Phoenix. My mind revved into overdrive as helpless seclusion made me feel a thousand miles away from any trace of civilization. I had drifted far enough away from my "safe area," leaving behind the security blanket of my shrinking prison.

Soon after passing the town of Tonopah, I started feeling detached and out of touch with my surroundings. My pulse was leaping in my throat. I struggled to recall where the nearest hospital was. Surely I was still close enough to a Phoenix hospital in case I needed medical help.

Turn around. I scanned the median between the westbound and eastbound lanes on the interstate looking for a clear area to turn around and head back to Phoenix—to Scottsdale, to my safety zone.

The phone was secured snugly between my legs with the map app engaged as I toggled my head every couple of seconds from watching the straight road out the windshield to gazing down at the crawling blue dot on the phone's GPS. With the map not zoomed in enough, it seemed I was progressing at an agonizingly slow pace. To disperse some nervous energy after I passed Exit 94, I yanked open the glove compartment and fumbled for the Arizona roadmap, thinking a paper map would somehow give the illusion of a shorter trip. After unfolding the map frantically and crinkling it into an erratic shape, I pushed it against the middle of the steering wheel and traced my route. The next exit wasn't for thirteen miles. I rammed my foot on the accelerator. The car downshifted then lurched forward, pushing the speedometer to just over a hundred. I attempted a mental calculation to determine how long it would take to arrive at the next exit at that speed. The numbers became a jumbled puzzle in my head as I extrapolated the less than ten-minute arrival time to Exit 81, the next exit. My lungs filled with air, but there was no comfort in it. I was not confident I could hold on that long. *But what if Exit 81 doesn't have a turnaround?*

Some exits in the middle of the desert didn't have a bridge allowing drivers to cross the interstate and head in the opposite direction. In all the times I had driven the route, I failed to memorize every exit—I would have to sink Exit 81 into my subconscious so I'd know next time if it had a bridge to reverse my course.

I psychotically blazed along the interstate playing this game with each exit. I passed Exit 81 thinking I could probably make it to the next exit, constantly scanning the hundred-foot-wide sparsely vegetated median for safe places to turn around—just in case. Exit 69, Exit 53, Exit 45, Exit 31, all their characteristics memorized now.

I did this mental dance all the way to Exit 17, the town of Quartzsite. Illuminating the now darkened desert sky, a lone gas station glimmered like some alien structure transmitting a welcome message.

As I put my credit card into the pay-at-the-pump slot and removed the gas cap, I worried about how I was going to make the trip all the way to Los Angeles without losing my mind completely. I could still turn around. I wasn't quite at the halfway point of the trip, which in my scabbed psyche was the scariest leg. It was the farthest point away from heading back to the safety of my home in Scottsdale, while also making it just as far to Los Angeles, a journey I didn't think I could bear to make in the first place. I felt stuck in the middle, hands cold and sweaty as I pumped gas into my car.

I drove over the bridge spanning the Colorado River into California, making my way to the mandatory stop at the California Inspection Station just a few miles past the border.

"Why are you traveling to California tonight?" the inspection clerk asked.

"For a visit with my family," I said, trying to collect upon myself a somewhat casual demeanor.

"Pleasure," he noted. "Are you carrying any fruits or vegetables with you?"

"Just a roast beef sandwich I packed with lettuce on it. Do you want me to throw out the lettuce?"

He scrutinized me for a moment before saying, "No, that's okay. Go ahead."

About twenty miles past the small town of Blythe, the back of my head began tingling. I looked apprehensively at the dark scenery looming around me. I started feeling like I was not real, just a floating molecule not grounded to anything. My eyes scanned the interior of the car in an attempt to produce some sort of comfort. *Here it goes again.* I glanced down at my legs and forced my tight grip on the steering wheel to slacken enough to inspect my left hand, putting the palm in front of my face and moving my fingers. I rolled my head around to study the car interior again in a desperate act to confirm I was really there.

There was a chilled bottle of spring water in one of the cup holders. I lifted the half-empty plastic bottle and poured the remaining clear liquid down my back, trying to feel the cold sensation. The water chugged out of the mouth of the bottle and soaked into my shirt fabric before slowing to a trickle at the bottom of my spine, but I registered no frigid reflex or sensation. Skin had somehow turned to tarp, an inanimate husk.

My visual acuity felt projector-like, my eyes playing a movie through me. It was a feeling of derealization—a disoriented equilibrium stripping away any sense of normal physiology. I put my index finger to my throat and clocked my heartbeat at a hundred-eighty. My body's bearing began to have the consistency of a lava lamp with my head being the little top blip of goo detaching from its skeletal base. As my lungs clamped tighter, I searched the black landscape hoping to see a hospital sign or a town nearby to comfort me with medical help.

Slipping slowly into cognizant shock, the overwhelming fears brought about an encircling darkness in my peripheral vision. Unconsciousness forthcoming, I jerked in my seat and slammed on the brakes, leaving a trail of smoking black rubber on the highway as my car came to a skidding stop just inside the reflective white shoulder line. A lone semi's horn blared as it blew past my car.

I exited the car and slammed the door. "Shit! Shit shit shit shit shit!" I shouted as I kicked the car's front fender while swinging my arms like a caffeine-laden jogger doing warm-up exercises. Then a glint of reality came when I looked around the darkness of the barren highway to see if anyone was watching me have a breakdown out in the desert. There were lights approaching from the other side of the interstate, but I was confident they did not see the kicking fit. My breath forced itself out of my mouth as I went to the other side of the car and started walking into the scrub about ten feet off the blacktop. I felt like running into the darkness until I collapsed and died, but I was too scared to venture away from the car and into the unknown.

I gazed westward, my eyes following the line of the road. My car's headlights were casting a beam on a large green highway sign sixty feet or so ahead. The exit to Palm Springs was thirty miles ahead. There would be a hospital in the area, but I knew upon arriving at a hospital, any hospital, I would suddenly feel at peace. Doctors would monitor my heart and give me a clean bill of health, sending me along with a bottle of pills and a few sheets of paperwork that would culminate in an outrageously bloated bill later. It had happened many times before. I was almost too scared to move, but in the drip of sanity that remained within me, I knew there was nothing else to do except to keep driving until I felt safe.

I got back into my car as my heart rate slowed, first looking to see if I had put any dents in the fender from my

Life Unbothered — Charlie Elliott

rapid kicks—I hadn't, but I did notice a scuff on my shoe. I sat down and ran my hands over the top of my water-dampened pants and shirt to straighten them out from the bottled water curative baptism earlier. I put the car in gear and revved the gas.

The lane lines of the interstate shot by like dashed clouds from a skywriting plane, and with no resounding pleasant memories to recall to keep me occupied, my focus settled on the origin of my altered life, a brief, seemingly innocuous event seven years ago that I would always remember with a sense of cemented permanence.

Without any warning, my life changed as a twenty-year-old junior in college on a regular day with a full regimen of morning classes. I was listening to a marketing lecture given by a lanky male professor in an ill-fitted suit whose hair rivaled that of the plasticized wigs worn by the eighties band Devo. As his lecture shifted to a discussion about color schemes on children's cereal boxes, a jolt sped up my spine and into my head, initiating the first panic attack I had ever experienced. The instant vertigo made me rise halfway out of my chair. Excruciating waves of pressure began pounding through my head like a red hammer. My heart rate doubled instantly, creating a pulsing splash in my ears. It felt as though I had morphed into a computer simulation, but I seemed to be the only one affected. The room started to spin as I scanned the four walls to see if any other of the thirty or so students felt the same dizziness I did, but their glazed eyes told me that I was in this alone. The girl seated to my left looked curiously at me, her blue eyes both questioning and concerned. Frozen in a half-standing position, I stared back at her. The blue smeared into the black and what had seemed to be concern, now looked more like pity.

I was dying, suffocating—I was immediately convinced of it. I wanted to run out of the room, but the fear of embarrassment kept me from doing so. I imagined myself collapsing on the carpet, gulping like a fish as my classmates stared at the freak on the floor. Terror becoming pure panic, I stood up, disregarding my lecture notes on the desk, and walked unsteadily into the hallway.

Breathe.
It's a heart attack.
Vessel popped. Stroke.
Can't breathe.
Keep walking. Get away.

Getting away. That's what my life became at that moment. Other episodes ensued as the attacks progressed into an unwelcomed habit. Standing in line in a grocery store, stopping at a red light in traffic, going to a movie, sitting in class. My affliction came with varying degrees of intensity, strengthening and receding like the four seasons. Despite my handicap, I managed to complete college, but when a job offer upon graduation led me to avoid the plane ride to Boston and therefore negating the offer, I knew the panic had taken over my life. I subsequently avoided other solid job offers; any trips that would take me to a career-furthering meeting; the woman or two who could have turned my life around—even the love of other people. I tried to keep it all at arm's length—anything that could have let me move forward—because that would have meant risk. Risk that I would panic—risk that others would *see* me panic.

Instead of going into corporate life, I decided to open an auto detailing business after graduation. Running my own business put me in control, shuttered me away from meetings with others and responsibilities I did not think I could fulfill. That was not the overt reason that I opened a business, but after burning out on cleaning cars and ultimately shutting the company down, I had come to the truth within myself as to why I started the business in the first place. No one knew the deeper truth in my entrepreneurial venture but me—it was all to avoid a normal life.

The doctors that followed over the years had assured me that no, I hadn't been having a heart attack or any other type of physical ailment. But they weren't in this body, hadn't felt what I had felt that day in the classroom and on thousands of occasions thereafter. The psychiatrists had their chance with me, pinpointing a diagnosis where the cause was undetermined and the cure was nebulous. Notwithstanding all the soft certainties of psychotherapy, for sanity's sake, I believed that I had no choice in the matter; internal chemistry had won out over contemplation.

My theory didn't help me procure a remedy, it just dulled the pain of what I had become.

Miles went by on the highway and the Palm Springs area passed by without a thought as I repeatedly assessed my life, from the day in college it started to all the induced misfortunes since. The pavement eventually grew wider as sparseness gave way to the expansive freeways of Los Angeles, but I was still shaken up from the drive through the desert. Mechanically, my body was fine. Changing lanes, applying the brakes, reacting to sudden traffic changes—all tasks I performed as if I were a typical driver. As I merged onto the perpetually busy Artesia Freeway about forty miles from my destination, I looked at other drivers gliding by, wondering what they were thinking about, if they knew the occupant one lane over from them wasn't thinking about the usual things: kids, bills, what to eat for dinner—rather he was a mere sliver away from leaving reality altogether.

I arrived in Palos Verdes just before eleven o'clock, astonished I had survived the trip. While I stretched my muscles back to normality in my parents' driveway, I tried to downplay the five hours of hell I had endured. The anxiety barbs settled back into their little crevices of my brain, resting up for the next opportunity to torture me. I was back in a safe place, the house of my parents, where I was accessible to help if needed. The overactive section of my brain's limbic system could now relax until the next trip—that's the testimony of control thoroughly engrained in my mind.

5. More Doctors

I stared out at the clear picturesque view of Los Angeles from my parents' laundry room window. Their house sat a thousand feet above the L.A. basin, providing a panoramic vista of the metropolis. Even the laundry room had a peak of city view that sliced the coast on a clear day all the way past Santa Monica. I was waiting for my travel iron to heat up so I could remove some wrinkles from my packed clothing. Though there was a very nice iron in the laundry room cupboard, I preferred my little fold-up travel iron because I knew exactly how much heat it took to do the job without searing the fabric or having to exert too much muscle to compress even the most subtle wrinkle. My mom entered the room as I flattened a polo shirt on the ironing board.

"Hi Wade," Evelyn said. "It's nice to see you on this surprise trip." Her voice always had a soothing quality to it, a sincere, friendly tone that came across in any circumstance. "Well, what's going on over in Arizona?"

I swiped my finger across the face of the iron to test the heat before responding. "Ummm, there's something I want—"

"Oh, before I forget, tell Pamela that I did get some purple orchids and gladiolas a little softer in color. I know her favorite colors are yellow and purple, but it nauseated the wedding planner to have those as the dominant color schemes. I have to admit, the liatris she loved looked like big purple pipe cleaners."

"Yeah, the colors were sick, unless you're a Louisiana State fan," I said.

"Well, she likes those colors and I want to have some of her favorites in the wedding. Out of the thousand-dozen flowers, she'll see some purple and yellow in there."

"You ordered twelve thousand flowers?"

"Oh, it's going to be beautiful," Evelyn said.

"Mom, I don't really want to talk about flowers right now. Where's Dad?"

"He's in his study."

"Can you get him? I want to discuss something with the both of you."

"Okay, just a minute."

I heard her shoes tapping down the long white marble hallway before she called out to Bob. Not knowing how to prepare the explanation of the wedding, I escaped for a moment with the iron, pressing the polo shirt with exacting strength. With each pass, the cloth became like a smooth sheet of fabric glass.

"He'll be here in a moment," Evelyn said upon returning to the laundry room. "Oh, and let Pamela know the gentleman from Colorado can get the white fantail doves to release after the wedding. I know she had her heart set on that."

Wedding blues were making a fleeting comeback as I rubbed my brow and closed my eyes.

"What the hell is the purpose of letting doves loose at a wedding?" I asked.

"Well… It's traditionally a sign of unity."

I squeezed the handle of the now hot iron and contemplated picking it up and running it across my face. "I don't see how hundreds of doves scattering in downtown Los Angeles signifies unity. I mean, where do they go?"

"I don't know Sweetie, but it will be lovely. Pamela really wants the doves at the wedding. It almost couldn't be done; we had to get some kind of a special permit to release them. Same thing with the horse and carriage."

I had forgotten about the carriage that was going to clog downtown traffic as Pamela and I trotted in our wedding best for an exuberant wee conjugal-exit jaunt around the block.

"Wade, my son. How are you doing?" Bob said as he walked into the laundry room.

"Um, not so good."

"You're not feeling well again, Sweetie?" Evelyn asked.

"Oh, probably just a case of cold feet," Bob said. "What's the matter?"

"Well, ummm... Pamela and I got in a little argument. Ultimately, I told her I didn't want to get married."

"Wade, I'm so sorry," my mom said. "Where is she now?"

"She found an apartment in Phoenix."

"What happened that was so drastic to cause this?" Bob cut in. He was always good at getting to the core issue.

"This has been brewing for a couple of months, Dad. I know I shut down my business at about the same time, but it really doesn't have much to do with that. She began to act bitchy about the wedding—how she wanted everything, from that stupid Bel Air dress designer to the limos for all her friends. Then she had the nerve to say after everything was finalized to *her* specifications, that she thought the reception would be too snooty. I just couldn't take it anymore."

"She said she wanted a *fairytale* wedding," Bob noted. "It's a shame she feels that way. But let me tell you, it's better to know now if she's not the right one rather than going through an unhappy marriage."

"Yeah, but you've spent all this money, most of it is probably not refundable. I feel like crap about that."

"Don't concern yourself for a second about the money." Bob's tone was just a step below irritation. "I'd rather you get away from a relationship that isn't right. The money spent doesn't mean a thing."

"But I just—"

"Wade, don't be troubled with the wedding," Evelyn interrupted and gently brushed my cheek. Fortunately, Pamela's morning phone-throwing incident did not leave a black eye or lingering marks. "It can all be canceled. You have enough on your mind right now."

"What about the damn doves?" I asked.

"Don't worry about the doves," my mom said with a slight chuckle.

"Are you absolutely sure you don't want to get married?" Bob asked.

"I've tried to feel differently, Dad. But I know Pamela is not the right one. I can't imagine spending the rest of my life with her. I already returned all the wedding gifts and snail-mailed letters to all our guests yesterday."

Putting it into an accommodating perspective, Bob said, "Well, Son, then I would say that you dodged a bullet."

"Yes I did," I said faintly, thinking about the gun to my head less than forty-eight hours earlier.

"Just go on, don't give the wedding another thought," he said.

Bob and Evelyn's attitude made the incident with Pamela manageable to escape from, untying at least one knot choking me. Deep in my mind I knew their reaction was going to be pretty much as how it happened in real time. My parents were always even-keeled and fair, which made it a comforting relief that I could somewhat transition from wedding to non-wedding in a mentally seamless manner. But in the end, it was easier for me to place emphasis on Pamela's shortcomings instead of addressing my own problems with forthright honesty--an undignified copout tugging further into my esteem.

As I finished ironing a polo shirt and started in on a pair of straight-legged pants, my dad left the laundry room while my mom stood across from me, obviously in meaningful thought. She always knew the deeper truth to life's challenges. I could never fool her.

"Do you think you should see a doctor again?" Evelyn asked in a sweet, concerned way only a loving mother could.

"None of them helped. This is a relationship problem, not a therapy concern. Anyway, some medication worked for a while, but the talking did nothing."

"I'm sure it seems that way to you, but remember Dr. Crouch? At least he's familiar with your condition. Don't sweep this under the rug, Wade. If you're having problems, go in and see him. Regardless of the situation with Pamela, it may be good to attend to other things you may be going through."

I had acquired a disdain of doctors, especially psychiatrists. They kept churning me through their therapy like a car on an endless assembly line, adding little tidbits and accessories to my psyche, yet never really completing the product. As I slid the iron over my pants, I figured Evelyn's cryptic suggestion had a point—and no other breakneck options came to mind.

* * * *

"So how does that make you feel?" Dr. Stanley Crouch asked as he twirled a tuft of thick mustache hair below his right nostril.

"Dr. Crouch," I grimaced, "what kind of a question is that? I need concrete solutions, not psycho-babble."

Keeping his head still, he glanced at me over the top of his glasses, then resumed looking at his notes. "Let's see, you initially saw me six years ago and last saw me two years ago. I also referred you to Dr. Leibostein in Phoenix. How did that go?"

"He really didn't help me. Just wanted to know about my childhood, et cetera. My childhood was fine, I need to know how to deal with the present."

"How many other doctors have you seen in the past six years?"

"About a half dozen."

"Okay." He paused and rubbed his nose. "I recall you also visited Dr. Smythe. What about his therapy?"

"Dr. Smythe? I remember him," I said. "He was into what he called, 'The natural path to healing your pain'. It wasn't effective."

"And why do you think that was?"

"Well, his treatment was *all natural*, so he prescribed a cocktail of remedies such as magnesium, gaba, kava, and some Internet sounding thing—HTTP3 or something."

"5-HTP," Dr. Crouch corrected me.

"You believe in that natural stuff too?"

"It has been shown to help some people, but it's not my normal path of therapy."

Dr. Crouch slumped in his worn high-back leather chair that had most likely been in his Beverly Hills office since he opened his practice about twenty years ago. Wavy, style-challenged sandy hair sat on his thin oval head like an oversized helmet. His languid body looked lost in the chair as his eyes darted between me and the memo pad on his lap.

"Did any doctors help you?" he asked.

"Not their talk therapy, but some of the medications did."

"Why did you stop taking them?"

"Because I thought I was better and didn't want them to eat my brain away."

"Wade," Dr. Crouch looked straight into my eyes, "you have an extensive history."

"I know but—"

"You have a severe case of anxiety disorder with panic attacks and depression." Dr. Crouch leaned forward. "Have you been having any obsessive traits or thoughts?"

"Besides worrying about going crazy, that's the only enduring theme. But I do like ironing my clothes a lot."

"Ironing," Dr. Crouch noted. "Is that affecting your life? I mean do you avoid things to iron?"

"No, I do it just for relaxation I guess," I said.

"Well, I didn't recall any obsessive-compulsive tendencies in our previous sessions, but watch for any ritual that goes beyond normal."

"I will. It's more of a relaxing obsession," I added.

"Have you had any scary thoughts?"

"Scary thoughts?"

"Thoughts of violence or hurting yourself?"

The scene in the desert with the gun played in my head, yet I didn't feel comfortable enough with Dr. Crouch to approach the subject, nor did I believe he could do anything about it. After recalling how close I came to splitting my head open with a bullet, I would not be trying to kill myself anytime soon, I hoped.

"No," I said.

Dr. Crouch consulted his notes while tapping his pen on the pad. "During your last visit, you mentioned having trouble traveling. Is that still the case?"

"Just flying," I answered with muted defensiveness.

"When's the last time you flew?"

"Three years ago—and it was a horrible flight. Panicked from the tarmac through to just before the landing. It was screwed up."

"Hmmm. Any other avoidances?"

"Well, I'm starting to not like traveling beyond a certain point at all, even by car."

"Is that getting worse?"

"Yes," I said with resignation.

"So you still suffer from agoraphobia. That's another one to put back on the list." He sighed and nestled deeper into his chair.

Agoraphobia. The dirtiest word in my vocabulary. The fear of open spaces, the terror of being detached. I felt it was more the fear of fear—which evolves into fear of everything ultimately. I rarely said it aloud and tried never to even internalize the word. It brought an immediate pang of anxiety just hearing Dr. Crouch say it.

"Have you experienced any particularly stressful situations lately?" Dr. Crouch asked.

"Yes… I guess. My fiancée and I just broke off our wedding due to irreconcilable differences."

"I see. Been there, done that. So how does that make you feel?" he said with a slight grin.

I gave him a thumbs-up and we both let out a chuckle. At least Dr. Crouch had a sense of humor integrated under his wavy hair. His comment helped dissipate the lingering definition of agoraphobia doing an ugly dance in my head.

"Well Wade, you have an extensive resume of treatments. You attended my group sessions in the past. How did you respond to those?"

"They made me feel better solely because many in your group were so much worse off than me. At least I've been able to remain somewhat functional. The sessions didn't really help—they just made me temporarily feel better through the misery of others."

Dr. Crouch lifted his pad to scan over old notes sitting on his lap. "I still think medication is the most viable path for you to stay stable."

"You mean I'm unstable?"

"No. It just seems you function better while on medication."

After a measured pause, I nodded sheepishly as an indication of agreement.

He fumbled again through sheets of paper. "Looking through your medication history—let's see, you've taken Ascendin, Norpramine, Lithium, Zoloft," he flipped to another sheet of paper, "Prozac, and the list goes on. Xanax seemed to be the most effective as I remember."

"Xanax was good for anxiety, it did help. But I didn't continue taking it because I knew it was addictive. I don't want to be on drugs all of my life."

Dr. Crouch's eyes narrowed slightly. "Maybe you should rethink your philosophy on that."

"You mean, actually take a drug for the rest of my life?"

"It's done all the time. People with heart trouble, thyroid problems, high blood pressure… many reasons."

"But this is for mental problems, not a physical condition."

"Consider this a lifelong physical disease. I'm going to put you back on one and a half milligrams of Xanax per day. Then I want you to return in two weeks." Dr. Crouch stood up, a cue our time was over. "I suggest you start learning more about your disorder so I can help you effectively."

He handed me the Xanax prescription. I nodded at his parting comment but held my breath to muzzle the immediate snap of anger that filled my body. I had read almost every book on the subject of panic disorder and probably knew more about the disease than some of the psychiatrists for whom I helped pay their country club dues, violin lessons for their kids, and Range Rovers for their pretty second wives. What I hadn't learned is how to successfully apply my studies to the subject.

6. The Intervention

Two days after my appointment with Dr. Crouch, I had yet to fill the Xanax prescription. The script remained neatly folded in half traveling about in my right-hand pocket, transferred day-to-day when I changed pants. My fingers rubbed the softening paper in my pocket as I entered the bar area of Poquito Gato, a popular Mexican restaurant located at the waterside of the Los Angeles Harbor. I was there to meet my ex-best man, Richard Haverport, for some drinks.

As I walked into the crowded bar area appropriately called the "Cantina," I spotted Richard and we exchanged a firm handshake followed by a quick masculine hug.

"Hey Wade. Isgood?" Richard asked in an upbeat tone.

"Isgood," I responded automatically.

Isgood was a slang term we invented in high school as a substitute for the more standard, "How are you doing?" Over the years it had just become another senseless greeting.

We sat at a window table overlooking the main channel of the harbor as container ships inched past filled with everything from household trinkets to advanced electronics, mostly from the Far East. A young waitress in a senorita-style miniskirt arrived to take our order when we sat down. I ordered a Crown Royal and water. Richard ordered a margarita.

"Got your email. Thanks for letting me know you aren't getting married," Richard said, sporting a shit-eating grin while he chewed on a flimsy cocktail straw. "How's Pamela?"

"Thanks for asking," I said facetiously. "She moved out of the house and into an apartment. We haven't spoken since then, and I don't plan to."

"Sorry to hear that."

I exhaled a laugh. "Right. You never liked her anyway."

"I know."

"Well, please make arrangements to call off any parties or activities you set-up. Sorry about all of this," I said.

Richard sighed. "That's okay, I'll take care of it. Too bad, we planned a great bachelor's party for you next week."

When the waitress came back, I took the glass directly from her tray and lifted it to my lips. The first biting sip made my mouth clamp like an over-tightened vise.

"So, Wade... what are you going to do now? Start another business?"

"I don't know... I'm dabbling in a couple of things."

I looked at Richard cautiously. Our close friendship hadn't wavered a bit since we met during our freshman year of high school. By the seriousness that flushed his face, I could tell he knew I wasn't the balanced package I was trying to present.

"Hey Wade, before you go off and do anything stupid, I'd like you to consider taking a job with my company. Marine engineering is a steady business. There will always be ships coming in and out of this harbor. My business is getting pretty big now and I need someone to handle things like insurance, benefits, payroll. You know, stuff like that."

"Thanks for the offer. Maybe later after I figure some things out."

"You must have something going on?"

"A couple of irons in the fire," I said with little conviction.

"Like what?" Richard prodded.

"Nothing big enough to talk about."

Richard set his margarita glass down and leaned over the table. "What the hell is wrong with you?"

"Huh?" I said, feigning surprise. "Nothing. I just called off a wedding. You know the one that was supposed to happen soon. I mean—"

"No, I'm not talking about the wedding with that dumb bitch. There are other things. For the past few years, it's as if you've disappeared or something. You backed out of our trip to Cabo last year. Before that, you missed skiing in Tahoe. I don't hear from you very often anymore—except for the wedding crap."

I fiddled nervously with a cocktail napkin as I heard the truth. It hurt to admit, but I had withdrawn from living, recoiling into my own cloistered world. I just didn't want to hear that fact from anyone else, even my best friend.

"Then when I talk to you, you don't seem the same," Richard continued. "Like you're dragging or bummed out. What the fuck is going on?"

"It's nothing, really," I said. "But you're right, I haven't felt like myself the past year. Maybe Pamela—"

"I hate to tell you this, Pal," Richard cut me off, "but you've been wigging even before Pamela. Yeah, that situation added to it, but something's been going on for a while."

As Richard finished his sentence, a big smile came across his face. He looked beyond me to the entrance of the bar area. I turned my head to see Scott Mundovich, another close high school friend and ex-groomsman. Scott, or Mundo as his friends called him, was my height and about thirty pounds heavier. The added poundage was not in fat, but muscle. His jet-black hair was short, flat on the top and shaved on the sides and back. A career Marine, he graduated from the University of Washington while enlisted in the ROTC program. He was a Captain based at Camp Pendleton, the Marine facility between Los Angeles and San Diego. I noticed his nonmilitary garb, a thick green t-shirt and olive pants loaded with cargo pockets splayed on the legs. One leg pocket had paper sticking out of the top.

I turned back to Richard as Mundo approached. "What's he doing here?"

"You need to be with some friends right now."

"Look, Richard, I said I didn't want to be with a bunch of people."

"Mundo!" Richard said as he stood.

"Hey Richard."

I lifted out of my chair slowly. "Hi Mundo."

"Wade," Mundo said as he compressed his husky arms around me, almost depleting the air from my lungs. "Great to see you." He stepped back and smiled. "Oh, and thanks for inviting me tonight, asshole."

"Well, I'm in town just for a short while and—"

"Yeah, don't feed me that," Mundo said. "Besides, we have a surprise for you." He looked at Richard. "You didn't tell him yet, did you?"

Richard's eyes shifted to mine. "No… I didn't tell him."

"What?" I said.

Mundo tapped his hand on the papers sticking out of his leg pocket. "We're going to Vegas."

"No we're not," I said.

"We thought since you made us all miss the bachelor's party, we'd just go to Vegas tonight to make up for it," Richard said. "It's in honor of your called-off wedding. May as well have some fun."

I looked at both of them as my chest muscles tightened and breathable air became a scarce commodity.

"Our plane leaves in a couple of hours, so drink up," Mundo said.

"Guys, I really appreciate this, but there's no way I'm going to Las Vegas tonight."

Richard grabbed my arm. "Don't be such a pantywaist. The three of us are going to Vegas. Forget about the rest of your drink. Let's go."

"Please don't do this to me. I can't go."

"Yeah you can," Mundo blared out as he navigated me through the rows of tables with a couple of well-placed nudges to my torso.

On the way to Richard's car, I could feel the adrenaline race straight to my head, creating the sensation of a balloon expanding inside my skull. Mundo and Richard were on either side of me, tucked in close.

"When are we coming back?" I asked my escorts.

"Don't know," Mundo answered. "It's Vegas. Maybe tomorrow, or the next day. Who cares?"

I looked at Richard. "What airline?"

"Festival," Richard said.

"Festival Airways? That's bargain basement. They don't even assign seats, it's festival seating. That's why they're named *Festival*. I think they still fly 727s, their fleet is ancient, the planes should be condemned to the Mojave jet graveyard."

"Wade," Richard said with an amused tone, "you've flown all around the world in worse shit than that. Las Vegas is a mere hour away. And Festival assigns seats now. They quit doing that run-to-your-seat thing years ago."

"Let me get some clean clothes out of my car," I said.

"You don't need any clothes, Wade. You look as sharp as ever with your creased pants," Mundo responded.

"What about my car? I don't want to leave it in the parking lot."

Richard looked at me knowing I was throwing out excuses. "Remember the owner of this place, Sammy?"

Richard pointed to the restaurant. "In case you forgot, we know the guy. He'll make sure your car is safe."

Mundo pushed me in the front passenger seat of Richard's Ford crew cab pickup, slammed the door and jumped in the back seat. I reached for the door handle as Richard was getting in the driver's seat. Richard grabbed my left arm as I began opening the door. From the back seat, Mundo cupped his hand forcefully around my right shoulder.

"C'mon Wade, don't try to get out of this," Mundo said.

I closed the door and looked at Richard. "What is this, some kind of guerilla intervention?"

"No, it's more a pleasure intervention," Richard said with a grin.

The drive to Los Angeles International Airport was a blur as the anticipatory anxiety built up steam and my thoughts overloaded with visions of being stuck in an aluminum tube suspended in the sky. I gazed out the window and watched cars beside us jockeying for lane position on the freeway. Richard and Mundo were speeding me away from the desires I yearned for, taking me to the airport—the equivalent of hell in my mind. It would be much more comforting to spend the night with an old girlfriend and engulf myself in her. That would be a shot of heroin for me, a blissful mindless escape.

"Where else would you rather be than with your friends going to Vegas?" Mundo asked.

"I was going to call Andrea and get together tonight," I said.

Mundo belted out a laugh. "Well then you can have a threesome with her hairball of a fiancé."

"She's engaged?"

"Getting married in June," Richard said.

"Shit, I thought she'd never get married," I said. "What about Cheri? I bet she would've spent the night with me."

"Wrong," Mundo leaned closer to my head from the back seat and yelled into my ear. "She's going to have a kid in a few months. You didn't know she got married last year?"

"No."

Richard smiled. "Face the reality, Wade. All your past admirers are married, or halfway through their first divorces."

"That's why we're going to Vegas," Mundo said. "There are plenty of chicks. You can pick one from those catalogs. They'll come right up to your room."

"Hell no. I'm not going to do that."

Mundo slapped the back of my seat. "I almost forgot. You're the pretty one. You never pay for sex."

"Oh I pay for it, just not up front."

"I still remember going out to bars with you before I was married," Mundo said. "The women would flock to you and I'd just sit alone and talk to myself. I was like the ugly cousin tagging along."

"You still are," Richard said. "Now you're just the ugly married cousin."

7. Puddle Jump

We'd like to welcome you to Festival Airways flight one forty-two with service to Las Vegas.

As the plane taxied to the takeoff line I tried to think of anything not panic-related, but my mind wouldn't allow it. Happy places and fond memories were doused quickly, replaced by terrifying images of going crazy—running down the aisle of a plane screaming. The air inside the plane was dense and my lungs struggled for nourishment. I sat stiffly in my seat afraid to move even a muscle. I was in the aisle seat, Mundo was in the middle, and Richard got the window. Vain attempts to dull my racing mental absorption were ineffective. I kept checking my shirt for newly formed wrinkles and brushed my hand over the fabric as if scattering dandruff.

"Relax Wade, this is going to be fun," Mundo cut in on my twisted thoughts.

"I'm not really liking this," I said.

"It's no problem. In an hour, we'll be in Las Vegas."

The hum of the engines grew to a steady roar and I sank back in my seat from the increased forward speed. The plane pitched upward and the floor rumbled as the landing gear curled into the fuselage. My legs began to quiver and a chill came upon me as the blood drained out of my extremities.

Emergency exits. Emergency exits! Where are the emergency exits?

I twisted my neck around to confirm the location of the emergency exits. The leap to freedom was about five rows behind me. I just wanted to know where they were in case I freaked out enough to pop one of the doors open and jump out.

As I tried to usher inner calm and rested my head against the seat back, my body lurched as if I had just suffered a seizure. It took a second for my mind to register the change, then a flood of all-encompassing dread came over me. It was panic unparalleled to anything I had ever felt, an instant attack of epic proportions. This attack felt like *the* one, a finalization of all the years of worrying. This horror was real, and there was nowhere to flee locked in an airplane—no escape.

I unclasped my seatbelt, jumped out of my seat and proceeded dizzily to the front of the cabin. I knew the emergency exits over the wings were behind me, but I kept heading for the front of the fuselage. I wasn't quite at the stage to attempt a fatal dive out of the plane—but I was close. I didn't know what kind of escape the forward section of the plane could offer, but my legs moved ahead, like a wild animal running instinctively from danger.

"Wade, sit down!" I heard Mundo's raised voice.

My outstretched hands touched every seat back as I continued down the aisle, trying to register the sensation of the cloth.

"DETACHED FROM THE GROUND!" I shouted as heads in front of me peeped out from the sides and tops of their seats all fixed on me, some with angry startled looks, others shocked. It surprised me as the words came out of my mouth.

"Detached from the ground," I repeated quietly to the gawking passengers as I stopped in the aisle.

It was my worst nightmare with nowhere to escape, embarrassing myself in front of an unfamiliar pack of people. I was so terrorized, I couldn't even blink my eyes. Exhalations made a loud whooshing sound as they exited my nose.

I stood petrified as two flight attendants walked up the aisle. When they got about five rows in front of me, the back of my body slammed to the floor and a crushing weight came down on my chest. I saw a man on top of me pivot his gouging knee to turn his body around while keeping me pinned to the floor. He jammed his hand around my neck as I started to pant wildly, gasping for air.

My attacker was a tanned, fifty-something freight train of a man with an overly round face covered by a couple days' worth of stubble. The thick black whiskers made their way almost to his eye sockets. His wide knee was so close to my face, I noticed the small weave patterns in his brown slacks.

"What the hell is your problem?" he blared.

I closed my eyes when his hot breath hit my face. As he removed his hand from my neck, I saw Mundo's blurred head dart behind the man. With a crushing blow, the man landed on top of me with force. Our faces collided before I could turn my head. The back of my skull immediately felt compacted. I imagined either some hair had ripped off my scalp, or I had just been dealt an unusually harsh back-of-the-head rug burn. Mundo's arms flailed wildly, jabbing into my ribs. He was on top of the man, doubling the weight on my already taxed lungs. A few seconds later the burden on my body lifted when Richard pulled Mundo off the man, alleviating half the weight on me.

I couldn't yet comprehend the ruckus of people gathering above as I remained with my back pressed against the aisle floor. Through a pair of legs, I could see Richard pushing Mundo down the aisle before disappearing behind the other bodies that were gathering for a closer look at the commotion. With Mundo gone, the man resumed his crouched position with one knee resting on my chest.

Richard reappeared, his head hovering directly above me. "Wade, you all right?"

I blurted out something that the best Freudian disciple probably couldn't translate. "My haunches are conflagrant." The words just flowed out of my mouth involuntarily. As I spoke, a young brunette stewardess from the front of the cabin knelt next to me.

"This guy is whacked out," the burly do-gooder said to the stewardess.

"Get off him," I heard Mundo shout from down the aisle.

The stewardess squatted beside me like a migrant worker taking a smoke break. Her legs were far enough apart to give me a birds-eye view of the pale pink panties underneath her knee-length polyester skirt. No pantyhose to haze the scene, just silky skin and double-lined cotton. The sight was comforting as I studied the soothing pink hue and soft creased skin. It would be the perfect place to bury the memory of this hideous incident, if I could only move my body. As the stewardess patted my left cheek gently, my speech was still uncontrolled.

"Your pink is swimming downstream," I said, lifting my right hand and pointing between her legs.

The stewardess recoiled her hand as if it had been bitten, clamped her knees together, and stood up. A male flight attendant quickly filled her place, crowding in between an aisle seat and my body.

"Do you have any sedatives or something?" the man with the heavy knee asked the male flight attendant.

"We don't carry any—at least not on a short puddle jump like this."

A blackish haze crept into my peripheral vision. My head lightened as an innate organic sedative flowed through me, administered by my own brain, overriding the terror. A synthetic tranquilizer would no longer be necessary. My body welcomed the impending darkness. I was flying in a benumbed state where all the people staring from above disappeared behind a black curtain and any trace of encroaching dread filtered away.

* * * *

Consciousness came back after what seemed like hours of sleep. I was still supine on the aisle floor and the scene was patently the same as it was when I left the world. Apparently I had only lost consciousness for mere seconds, the same faces were still gawking down at me as I rolled my eyes around the circle of people.

"Can you hear me?" the male flight attendant said, enunciating all four words.

"Yes," I grunted.

"Wade, you want to stand up?" Richard asked.

"Yeah."

"What's the matter with you, boy?" the man who tackled me said.

His knee was still on my chest, but he had shifted most of the weight to the other leg, giving me some relief. I took in a couple of fast breaths as my body wound down a bit and my head regained its equilibrium.

"I'm just scared of flying. I had a panic attack."

After I had said it, I realized it was the first time I had ever admitted having a panic attack to strangers—and even to Richard. It was like confessing to a crime that I had committed years ago. It felt good to get it off my shoulders—I just never expected to do it on my back in the aisle of a commercial airliner.

"A panic attack?" The man removed his knee from my chest and sighed. "Jeez, that's it? I was a volunteer sky marshal for a while. I thought you were a terrorist or something. You scared the crap out of me."

"No, no terrorist here. It's more of a personal issue thing," I said.

The man grunted and slowly rose to his feet. He grabbed my right arm and Richard grabbed my left. They pulled me up so fast I became dizzy as blood drained out of my head. Standing provided a full view of the plane's interior. I tried not to look around at the crowd of people gawking in my direction. My hands furiously went to work on the creases of my pants, trying to undo the ruffles created when the man tackled me. I looked up and glanced at Richard, whose eyes were wide, as open as I'd ever seen them.

"Come on Wade, let's go sit back down," Richard said.

"I'll sit next to him," my attacker said to the flight attendant.

The flight attendant looked at Richard. "I think it would be better if you just went back to your seat. We'll take care of, what's his name? Wade? We'll take care of Wade up here."

"It's okay Richard, just go back to your seat and calm Mundo down." I pointed to the seat next to me, about ten rows up from where Richard and Mundo were sitting. "Nobody's sitting in this seat, I'll just sit here."

The man directed his attention to Richard. "Your friend who jumped on me, tell him sorry. I was just trying to control the situation."

"He'll understand. He just doesn't like people tackling his friends," Richard said with a grin.

I slumped low in my new seat, knowing that I was the most embarrassed person on the plane by a long shot. The ex-marshal took the empty middle seat next to me. I vied for more armrest room with a couple of subtle nudges to his thick forearm. His arm didn't move. My breathing calmed down enough to hear some whispered conversations going on around me. *"What's the matter with him?" "Did he try to hijack the plane?" "Does he have a bomb?"*

"I'm sorry, I just kind of lost it for a minute," I said to the man.

"It happens," he said. "But I suggest you don't fly for a while. At least not on any flight I'm on."

To my dismay, the male flight attendant returned a few minutes later and demanded some personal information to include in his report of the incident. The plane didn't appear to make any sweeping turns, so I assumed we were not reversing course back to Los Angeles. I relinquished my Arizona driver's license reluctantly and assured him that the information was accurate. The address was wrong. I didn't care to tell him. My main concern wasn't the airline's report, but rather the possibility of arrest and detainment when I arrived in Las Vegas.

Time seemed to speed up as I sat staring at the tray table in front of me tucked neatly in its upright position. Before I knew it, the plane tipped downward to start its descent. It was a short flight, but one that was now etched into my memory of towering negative events.

I didn't speak again to the gentleman who saved the plane from my raving lunacy. I didn't even bother to get his name. The only words spoken were from the male flight attendant who instructed me to stay in my seat upon landing until every passenger had deplaned. I just wanted to run when the doors opened but would have to delay that plan. After the plane touched down, the man in the middle seat abruptly wedged by me and went to the front while we taxied to the gate.

Ding. The humiliation set in as the seatbelt sign chimed and passengers in front of me glared back to get one last look at the crackpot, while those from behind turned their heads toward me as they passed by my seat. I wanted to give a courteous smile to the rubberneckers, but I was too ashamed to make any hint of eye contact. I continued looking down at my lap as I let the people pass, not wanting to stand and be ogled like some kind of criminal on a perp walk.

"Okay Wade, let's get out of here," Richard said as he sidled my seat after there were no other passengers remaining.

Mundo put his hand on my shoulder as I stepped into the aisle. "You all right?"

"I'm just worn out. Sorry about the commotion."

I proceeded to the front of the plane as inconspicuously as possible, despite the tiny prickles of sweat coming from my skin that felt like steamy spotlights were aiming their beam down on me. About fifteen feet from the door, my gateway to freedom, I saw the man who tackled me talking to another guy, while the male flight attendant who confiscated my license eagerly pointed my way. The stewardess I had offended by commenting on her panties turned quickly and scurried down the walkway. Another man holding a walkie-talkie singled out Richard and Mundo and led them down the walkway, leaving me alone in the plane.

"Mr. Hampton?" asked the man I had never seen before. His "service with a smile" expression made me pause for a moment before I nodded in recognition.

"I'm Brent Howe, head of security for Festival Airways in Las Vegas. How are you?"

"I had kind of a rough flight," I said.

"Could you please follow me?" Brent gestured to the plane hatch as the former sky marshal passed us and disappeared down the walkway.

I followed Brent Howe and the male flight attendant to the terminal. We made an immediate right turn after disembarking and settled behind a small unused ticket counter near the gate. The walk seemed as if it took an hour as my legs stiffened from the fear. Although I was relieved to be off the plane, anxiety still burned in my gut as I worried about going to jail. I didn't think I could survive being restrained twice in a night with nowhere to escape.

Brent turned around to face me. "Mr. Hampton, we received a report that you caused a disturbance on flight one forty-two, the flight you just deplaned." My mind was defogging, but I was still a little slow and remained silent while he waited for an explanation. "Do you want to tell me about that?" Brent asked finally, a bit insistently.

"I'm really sorry. Look, I was getting married and under some stress. I just flipped out for a moment."

"Oh, congratulations," Brent said, though it sounded disingenuous. "Wait, was your wife also on the plane, or is she already here in Las Vegas?"

"No, she's in Phoenix. And she's not my wife." I looked at him as if he should've already known that. "I was on the plane because I think my friends know I'm afraid of flying."

Brent and the flight attendant turned to each other in puzzlement. It then dawned on me how strange the dialogue must have sounded.

Brent lifted his hands. "Now let me get this straight—" he paused to start on a different track, deciding not to risk an elaboration. "Whatever the case may be, since there was no damage caused or threats made by you and your upheaval didn't delay the flight, we have decided not to take further action against you."

"Thank you."

"Do you have a connecting or return flight with us at Festival Airways?"

"Not that I know of."

"Great. The only thing we at Festival Airways ask is that you refrain from flying with us anymore. Can you do that?"

"I don't think that'll be a problem."

"Good. Thank you and have a nice evening."

Brent nodded to the flight attendant, allowing him to relinquish my driver's license. He imparted an unnatural smile as I lifted my limp hand to retrieve the license.

After the two walked away, I saw Richard and Mundo in the middle of the terminal. They were talking to a small group of Fed types and a cop from the Las Vegas Metropolitan Police Department. I didn't feel stable enough to walk over to join them, so I stood frozen in front of the empty ticket counter and waited for the outcome of their meeting.

8. The Tightrope

When their meeting with security was over, Richard and Mundo approached me as I stood in place, cemented to the floor.

"What do you want to do now?" Mundo asked.

"I want to go home," I said in a shaky voice.

"Let's do a little gambling. It'll get your mind off the plane ride. You'll feel better once we get to a casino."

"No, Mundo," I said. "I want to go back to Los Angeles."

"Come on Wade, you made it here. Yeah, maybe with some setbacks, but we may as well have some fun."

"Shut up, Mundo," Richard bellowed. "Wade, we'll do whatever you want. You want to go back to L.A.?"

"Yeah, I really do."

"Let's just go to a hotel—"

"Mundo!" Richard's eyes intensified. "Wade, do you want to fly back right now?"

"No, I don't want to fly. Anyway, I'm not allowed back on Festival Airways."

"Me neither," Mundo broke in. "The security guys told me I violated like fourteen Federal laws on the plane and I was lucky they weren't going to haul me to jail."

"Yeah, I know," Richard said. "Let's just get a rental car."

"That would be a lot better," I said.

We headed over to a row of car rental booths by the passenger ticketing area. Richard stopped walking about twenty feet from the Swifty Rent-A-Car counter.

"Stay here with him. I'll get us a car," Richard said to Mundo.

Mundo and I waited in silence as I attempted to remain as incognito as possible, not wanting to chance being noticed by anyone on the flight as passengers milled by. A lukewarm sickness arose in my stomach knowing that the flight had done irreversible damage. Perhaps years, even decades of airline avoidance engrained in the centermost crevasse of my soul. Maybe getting married to someone I didn't love was an easier option than taking a forced flight with friends. No, it couldn't be true, but the intensity of the moment made it feel as such. I stared at the back of Richard as he signed off on the rental car, but in actuality, I was staring at nothing. Shock was sweating itself off my body and my brainwaves turned nil as I waited. This was the common post-panic stage, body chemistry was diligently trying to rebalance itself.

"Okay, I got a car," Richard said when he returned. "We can go outside and get the Swifty shuttle to take us to their lot."

"You paid for a one-way rental?" I asked.

Richard paused for a second and shifted his eyes over to me. "Well, not exactly. I failed to tell the agent that we didn't plan to return. I figured we could deposit the car at an outlet in L.A."

"I don't think you can do that," I said. "I don't want you to get in trouble on account of me."

"Wade, you're the one who taught me that 'one-way' trick. Remember when we were skiing in Colorado and picked up that rental in Denver, but the snow was better in Utah so we spent a day driving the car over to Park City?"

"Yeah, I remember." I tried to smile, recalling the good time.

"Well, you did the same thing at the rental place. That was a local rental, but you ended up dropping the car at the airport in Salt Lake City." Richard looked at the well-traversed tile floor before he continued. "Now you're worried about something like that? Shit, things have really changed."

I stared off beyond Richard and sank a bit in my shoes as it hit me how much I had changed. Just going to a bordering state assumed the form of a neurotic disaster.

"Guys, there's the Swifty shuttle," Mundo said as he pointed outside toward the passenger pick-up area.

After a short shuttle ride to the Swifty lot on the outskirts of the airport, we located the white Chevy SUV rental. Under the bright lights of the parking lot, my body cooled and goosebumps rose on my forearms. The night sky was clear and the temperature hovered in the low sixties. My skeleton still felt shaky, but the relief of knowing we were en route back to a safe place brought on additional mental and physical stability.

"I'll drive," I offered as we approached the car.

"No, I'll drive," Richard said.

"It's okay, I *can* drive. I just didn't like the flight."

"I know you can drive. I'm the only one registered on the rental, so I have to drive."

"I don't care who drives, just so it's not me," Mundo said. "I want to stretch out in the back. How long of a drive is it anyway?"

"Probably about five hours or so," I said.

Mundo jumped into the back seat. "Well then stop at a store on the way out of town and pick up some beer."

Richard navigated the SUV around the Vegas traffic and stopped at a Horrible Hearst convenience mart just before the onramp to I-15. We all got out of the car and went to our respective places in the store. Mundo opted for a twelve-pack of Coors, I grabbed a twenty-ounce bottle of Diet Coke without caffeine, Richard got a bottle of water and some sunflower seeds.

We proceeded to get on the interstate and roll out of Las Vegas, almost as fast as we had landed on the flight earlier. I fiddled with the satellite radio and the GPS while Mundo enjoyed a cold beer, placing it between his legs during gulping sabbaticals. As the road gained altitude about twenty miles outside the city, the brightness of the Las Vegas skyline reflected through the side rearview mirror. I looked in the sky above Las Vegas and saw the tiered pattern of lights from airplanes on approach to McCarran Airport. I couldn't imagine anyone on those approaching flights ever feeling like I did—the fear, the physical reactions, the enclosure of the cabin.

As we passed through the first set of barren hills, eventually all that remained of the city was the light shooting skyward from the top of the Luxor Hotel pyramid, the brightest beam in the world. Las Vegas was vanishing.

"Wade, you want a beer?" Mundo asked from the back seat.

"No thanks."

"Are you all right now?" Richard asked.

"Yeah, I'm fine."

Richard turned his head to me. From the corner of my eye I could see a bluish tint on his face from the dash lights.

"You sure you're fine? I mean, what the hell was that back there on the plane?"

"I just don't like flying," I said.

"Don't like flying? Shit, Wade, freaking out like that is a little more than not liking flying. What the hell is wrong with you?"

"I guess my mind hasn't been right for a while," I admitted. "I feel detached. Like when I go somewhere, my head doesn't feel right."

"What do you mean?"

I hesitated elaborating, but these were two of my best friends. Guys I'd keep in touch with for the rest of my life, no matter where our paths went, or how many years between contacts.

"I feel like I'm walking a tightrope, some high-wire act from hell. You know?"

"I don't know what you just went through on that plane, but you know what? Quit being so mellow and downplaying this, and stop talking like some political asswipe. Tell me what's going on with you—in English."

We looked at each other. I could see the seriousness in Richard's eyes, and it seemed he could discern the sadness in mine. I decided to come clean. Outside of my family, Richard and Mundo were the two best people to explain what I was going through. I gathered my thoughts for a moment as I glanced out the car window into the darkness.

"Well, I've become fearful of flying over the past few years. I get in a plane and I have a panic attack."

"I get nervous when I get on a plane," Mundo said.

"No, it's different than just nervous, it's like uncontrollable terror."

"Yeah, I'm scared sometimes in my life, but I learn to deal with it."

I turned my head to Mundo. "It's not about getting scared. It's about signals firing in my head that don't make rational sense. What the hell do you care about it anyway? Just enjoy your beer."

"What the hell do I care?" Mundo leaned his oversized head forward to fit in between the front seats. "I'm getting transferred at the end of the month to Camp Lejeune in North Carolina. I have to move my family out there. I was supposed to be transferred earlier, but delayed it until after your wedding."

"I didn't know you were being transferred."

"No shit. You've been such a hermit lately, nobody talks to you anymore."

"Mundo, I'm sorry," I said.

"I don't mind the transfer, but it does piss me off that you don't think I care. Hell, Wade, everyone cares about you. Richard and I both got liberty passes from our wives to take you to Vegas tonight. Of course the bachelor party we had planned would have been a tougher sell to my wife. But since we heard about the canceled wedding, everyone has been concerned. That's how much we all care."

I stared at him a moment, not knowing what to say.

"So explain to us what's going on," Mundo said. "I know you just think I'm a dumb jarhead, but at least try."

"Yeah, tell us," Richard requested.

I sighed, then started my explanation. "Well, what I have is panic disorder, or at least that's what the doctors call it. It's some kind of mental condition that causes unprovoked bouts of severe anxiety and fear for no obvious reason."

"What does it feel like?" Richard asked.

"You know like when you're in a dangerous situation and your body starts reacting?"

"Yeah."

"Let's say you're walking down a sidewalk and an out-of-control semi truck came barreling directly at you. Or better yet, the truck is trying to run down Mundo."

"Thanks," Mundo said sardonically.

"When you see the truck, a reaction occurs in your body. A fight-or-flight response kicks in."

"Fight or flight," Richard noted. "I've heard of that."

"Yeah, it's a survival mechanism in all of us. In most cases, unless you're suicidal or on crack or something, you wouldn't remain on the sidewalk as the truck approaches closer, or fight it, so the flight response kicks in to produce the physical ability to jump out of the way to safety. That's why when you're scared, your adrenaline flows, your breathing increases, there may be trembling… all products of fight-or-flight. The aftermath is a natural ingrained avoidance of getting in the way of semi-trucks, along with most similarly dangerous situations."

"Yeah, but that fight-flight thing is healthy, it keeps you alive," Mundo noted.

"True, it is healthy," I agreed. "But imagine you're in a restaurant with your wife eating a leisurely dinner when the same reactions arise—like the semi-truck was about to run you down. There's no danger present, but the same physical and mental reactions occur for no distinct reason. After repeated episodes, all of a sudden your brain tells you, 'hey dumb-ass, don't go into restaurants'. So you avoid them."

"You're scared of restaurants too?" Mundo asked.

"I've avoided them in the past, but it's only out of the fear of having a panic attack. It's not like I truly think restaurants are dangerous."

"Well some are. You should have gone with us to that chorizo place in Harbor City a couple of weeks ago. It almost gutted me," Richard said.

"Serves you right," I said. "But the avoidance can grow to other things. In severe cases, some people are so consumed by panic attacks they haven't left their house for over a decade."

"No way, I don't believe it. How long have you suffered from this?" Richard asked.

"From what I can tell, it started in college."

"Yeah, I figured that. You seemed like you started getting depressed while we were in college."

"Depression has been a byproduct of this. The panic attacks can induce phobias that lead to depression. It's like having a physical handicap that cycles in and out."

"I just don't understand what you're going through," Richard said as his hands fiddled to reset the cruise control to a faster speed.

"I know it makes no sense to you."

"All I remember Wade, are things like that trip we took to Europe and Africa eight years ago. Remember that guy we paid twenty bucks to show us how to get to the top of one of the Great Pyramids without getting caught?"

"Yeah, we had to wait until after midnight, after the touristy light show to climb up to the top."

"I still have that picture on my wall. The one taken the morning we woke up on top of the pyramid at sunrise."

"I wonder what would have happened if we got caught up there spending the night. That guy who got us to the base of the pyramid was all paranoid," I said.

Richard laughed. "We could've gone to an Egyptian jail. That was the same trip we took that ferry from Spain to Morocco just a couple of days before."

"Yeah, I remember. Our passports were pulled and we got locked up in that cement room for twenty hours."

"You got locked up in Morocco?" Mundo asked.

"More like detained. We happened to pull into Tangier the day of a government coup attempt," I explained. "It was just bad timing on our part. But they gave us our passports back and we got the hell out of Tangier and took a train down the coast to Casablanca."

"That was the greatest trip I ever took," Richard said.

"Yeah, that was a good one."

"I just can't believe you're the same person. I mean, an hour flight and you freak out?"

"I know," I said with resignation.

I sat silently for a while, mesmerized by the road as I reminisced about Arizona. I had been there for nine years through college and my stint as a mediocre businessperson. After the plane ride, it was obvious I couldn't lead a normal life if I continued burrowing myself into an inky grotto of instability. Change was needed.

"Hey Richard, you really serious about the job you offered?" I asked.

"Wade, it'd be great if you were to move back to California and come work at my company. I mean, you can work on this panic problem at the same time. I think you should get away from Phoenix and come back."

"I guess you're right. I'll come back and work for you… and thank you for the offer. I just wish I could have flowed into society without a hitch like you and many other friends. Everyone's married, getting careers, going places. I'm having a hard time establishing anything."

"Promise me two things," Richard said. "Don't claim to be a victim, and quit feeling sorry for yourself." He stared at me intently with wide eyes. "I just hope you're not trying to shit on your doily."

"Shit on what?"

"Your doily," Richard answered. "It's something a few of us made up one drunken night to describe some of our friends from high school. You know, we all grew up in a nice area, most of us came from families with parents who work hard and make a decent amount of money. Our lives were kind of like doilies, nice and pressed—like your pants always are. Some guys really fucked that up when they got out into the real world."

"No, Richard, I'm not trying to soil my doily in the least. I just have some mental challenges that are affecting my life. It's like there's some corrupt *bling bling* in my brain, fat gold chains of despair wrapped around my genes."

"Well, you better cut those chains or life may be over, my friend."

"Thanks for the advice. I'll work out the details and timing for me to move back. I'll get rid of the house and move my stuff over later this month. I have to be back for a doctor's appointment in a couple of weeks. How about if I start after that?"

"That's fine. I'll make it worth your while," Richard said, as we knocked knuckles to seal the deal.

Some sounds came from the back seat. Mundo's head was bobbing to the flows of the rental car's suspension. It took only half the twelve-pack to do the job. I tapped Richard's arm and directed my eyes to the back seat.

"Typical Mundo. He always goes out like a light in a car," I said.

9. The Return

We arrived home just before four in the morning after a hazy-headed, yet panic-tolerant drive from Las Vegas. After the first hour, the drive was fairly uneventful. It beat worrying insistently about the location of the next road exit. My brain was too tired from the flight and had to wind down. I decided to spend the rest of the short night sleeping at Richard's house so we could return the rental SUV the next morning and retrieve his truck at LAX.

We woke up at about nine and Richard drove me to pick up my car at Poquito Gato where I had left it the night before when Richard and Mundo kidnapped me. The restaurant was closed, and my car sat alone in the parking lot.

I followed Richard to the Swifty Rent-A-Car lot on El Segundo Boulevard, in close proximity to the Los Angeles International Airport. Richard went through the drop-off procedure while I stayed in my car. I tilted my head back and let the sunrays soak my face. The warmth was relaxing, but it didn't strip away my sullen mood. I was embarrassed of what I had become and ashamed I had ruined the trip with Richard and Mundo. The flight had further stripped my esteem of any sense of traveling adventure. I believed my current passport would expire with no other country stamps, except for the two dozen that were already in there. What about the states within this continent? I had been to forty-five of them—would I ever see the other five? Would my feet ever reach the soil in Alaska, Iowa, Nebraska,

North Dakota or Vermont? I hoped the incident on the flight was the bottom of the emotional curve and some kind of reversal of fortune would breathe new life into me.

"Okay, let's go get my truck," Richard said as he entered the car.

"How much did you have to pay for dropping the car three hundred miles off-course?" I asked.

"Not too much. Just a service charge."

"Let me at least pay the hijacking charge. You wouldn't even let me pay for the rental car last night."

"No Wade, that's okay. Consider it a non-wedding present. I'm glad you're not going to marry her anyway."

I nodded and contemplated a smart-ass response, but decided to let the comment speak for itself.

As I drove Richard to the concrete parking structure in the middle of LAX, the overwhelming desire to waste away in a woman's arms for the day occupied my thoughts, but none were available. All the reliable standbys in California had forged new lives and outgrown the need to accommodate the shallow sexual relationship I offered. It was time to return to Arizona and wrap things up.

When I stopped in the parking terminal by Richard's truck, he unbuckled his seatbelt and patted my shoulder. "See you in a couple of weeks."

"I'll be there," I said, making a valiant effort to exude self-confidence. "And thanks again."

I drove back to my parents' house via Pacific Coast Highway, taking in the calming ocean breeze before I put my body through another journey back to Arizona. My mom and dad weren't home, so I stripped naked and ironed the clothing I was wearing while admiring the view of Los Angeles from the laundry room window. Then the iron went to work on every piece of clothing in my bag. I put back on the clothes I was originally wearing instead of changing into a new outfit altogether. The drab earth-tone garb seemed refreshed enough for me to feel comfortable even though the outfit had been flattened on old airplane aisle carpet from the night before. I wanted to look well put together and not too strange if I had an emergency on the road and needed help from a stranger. Nice and unthreatening, but not too dressed up to look entitled. I wouldn't want to be stuck on the road looking too good for the fear no one would come to my assistance, like I had it all put together and didn't need anything from some sympathetic outsider. Except for the BMW I was driving, the personal look suited the possible help-mode scenario.

    I left my parents a note telling them I was going back to Phoenix. Before heading to the freeway, I stopped at Osco Drugs to fill the Xanax prescription. My medication procrastination couldn't wait any longer. I needed something besides freshly pressed clothing to help me cope during the drive back to Phoenix.

    "Wade Hampton," I said to the attractive Hispanic pharmacist as Osco Drugs. I spied a good view of her as she turned around and bent over to fetch my prescription out of the "H" bin. Her clinical white outfit draped nicely over her sumptuous curves.

"Here you are," she said with a friendly grin.

I tried to generate my most charming smile, but it always felt contrived whenever I attempted it. Like my mouth was an actor playing the role of its career.

"Thank you," I said.

I studied the prescription bottle as I made my way out to the parking lot. I stopped by a trashcan to tear up the irritating disclaimer sheets. I didn't care what it had to say, the possible side effects, what the drug was commonly prescribed for—I already knew all of that. Though millions of people from all walks of life take the drug, I tore up the sheets because I didn't want anyone to see my name on a prescription for Xanax.

I sat in my car and dumped one pale orange half-milligram pill in my hand, studying it intently, wondering if I really needed the stuff. With the exception of Xanax being addictive, I was not opposed to the medication in general. It just irritated me that once again I was going back on an antidote—this time to get me to Phoenix. I lifted my palm and tossed the pill into the back of my mouth, then swallowed hard. I was still worried about the anticipated hell I was about to go through and popped another pill in my mouth as I merged on the Harbor Freeway.

An hour into the trip, I was almost calm enough to enjoy the drive. A low-frequency buzz was keeping my anxieties at bay. With a completely empty stomach aiding the absorption of the drug, it allowed me to wheel down the freeway just like any other average medicated schmo. Some old Primus was blaring on the digital player as my car glided into the fringes of the desert.

I decided to call some females in Phoenix to see if I could set up something for the night. Being out of extensive casual lovemaking circulation since Pamela moved in, except for my neighbor Colleen, I wanted to reconnect with those who went astray when Pamela arrived.

First on my call list was Stella Waters. She was always up for anything when we were together. I pressed the call button, placed the phone to my ear, and then shifted my eyes back to the road.

"Hey Stella, this is Wade."

"Wade? Wade Hampton?"

"Yeah. How's it going?"

"I thought you were getting married? Like soon."

"No, it's not happening. I was wondering what you were doing tonight."

"What do you have in mind?" Stella asked.

"Maybe you can come over, you know?"

"You want me to come over? Where's your fiancée?"

"No. You see, I'm not getting married. It's over," I said.

"You're not getting married? Why?"

"I guess the timing wasn't right."

"You're really not getting married?"

"Nope."

A lingering sigh from Stella indicated a coming change in her tone of voice. "Wade, I'm sorry. I'll always love you, but you checked out on me months ago."

"Well that's why I'm calling—to check back in."

"You know, I have a steady boyfriend right now and we're getting pretty serious. I'd love to be with you, but I just can't."

Proceeding down my phone list, I began to feel like a cold caller peddling rotten steaks to unsuspecting senior citizens. I called Brenda, Kimberly, Paige, Cameron, Erin, Catherine, and Samantha to no avail. Two numbers were disconnected, one a man answered, and the rest didn't answer. I also phoned Ashley, but got some sickening voicemail greeting: *"Hi… this is Ashley… and this is Brad… and we're not home!"* I hung up. The only message I left was to my neighbor Colleen—then I gave up.

As I approached the halfway point of the drive just west of Blythe, the Xanax felt like it was starting to wear off and my thoughts drifted to the agoraphobic side.

Out in the middle of nowhere.

Before I slipped into full panic attack mode, I decided to make one more call in an attempt to divert the inevitable. I scrolled through my phone list to find Pamela's cell phone number. As a guise, I wanted to show a sliver of courtesy by telling her that I was moving to California, but the primary reason for the call was to keep my mind occupied as I spanned the open highway.

"Hello?"

"Hi Pamela, it's me… Wade."

A pause ensued. I didn't know if it was the cellular connection or if she was getting her anger revved up.

"Oh, hi," she said stiffly. "Where are you?"

"I'm kind of by the Arizona border. I've been in L.A. for a few days."

"Why? To complain to your parents about me?"

I had to adjust my breathing and slow down the inhalations so my voice wouldn't shake. "Come on, Pamela. No, I didn't complain about you. I barely saw them."

"Then why did you go out there?"

"Just to get away, I guess. What are you doing?"

"I was supposed to meet with that private shopper your mom got me to find a honeymoon outfit, but someone didn't want to get fucking married. So now I'm sitting in my apartment exfoliating my feet to heal the blisters I still have from when you abandoned me in the desert."

"Oh, okay. I was just calling to see how you were."

"Screw you, Wade. It's a little late for that."

I swallowed to adjust my vocal chords to a pleasant tone. "Hey, uh, I've got some news. I'm moving to California." I closed my eyes as I told her, anticipating a blaring devil to erupt out of the phone.

"You're what?"

"I'm—"

"You are moving to fucking California?" The phone rattled a bit, but at least the *devil* was a couple of hundred miles away. "Just like that, you're moving. I don't fucking believe you."

"What are you so mad about? We're not together anymore. You've moved out, you think I'm nuts. Why are you mad?"

I asked, though I knew the answer. It didn't matter that she hated me, she wanted to be married. It didn't happen.

"I can't believe you, Wade. So just like that, you're moving to California. That's just great."

"I took a job over there, that's why I'm moving."

Pamela had never really fathomed, even in the last weeks we were together, to what degree the panic disorder had taken over my life. My panic, depression, agoraphobia and cousin ailments were the reason I got engaged to her in the first place, and the reason I called off our wedding—and ultimately the reason behind moving. She never realized mental illness guided most of my important decisions. I didn't expect her to comprehend my problem. No normal person seemed able to either.

"There are jobs here, you know."

"But this one is better than any I've been able to track down here," I lied, knowing I hadn't exerted any effort in a job search.

"So you're going to move, just like that," she said, more resigned. "When?"

"Next week."

"Next week?" Pamela brought her voice up to a tone I was readily familiar with. "You're moving next week and just now decided to tell me?"

As Pamela pecked away at me, I thought about us being married. I pictured her thirty years in the future with dyed frazzled hair and weighing about three hundred pounds, waving a dough roller daily at my head as a right bestowed to her as my wife.

"I just learned about this job yesterday."

"Well I'm glad you're having such a great fucking time. Who is it? Some little skank you're moving out there to screw?"

"No, Pamela, I'm not moving out there for a girl. I got a damn job."

"Oh screw off, Wade. Go ahead and move to L.A. That's wonderful, I'm very happy for you. Just for that, I'm keeping the ring."

"Pamela," I said in a more soothing tone, "it'll be all right—"

Click.

Pamela hung up the phone. I would have to gut the rest of the drive in agoraphobic fright.

Exit 17, Exit 31, Exit 45, Exit 53, Exit 69. For the remainder of the trip, I tried to focus exclusively on the conversation with Pamela. I went so far as to imagine her tending to her foot blisters, the skin shavings drifting into her new apartment carpet. From there, the dead skin became sustaining food for dust mites, eating a former part of Pamela. I traveled into the underworld of the carpet and imagined a family of dust mites having a danderous time chomping on bits of dry skin before going off for some entertainment later. Perhaps taking their dust mite kids, bellies full of Pamela's toe skin, to an errant polyester carpet fiber that serves as a big slide to delight the youngsters.

I tried to keep my visions within the carpet, creating alternate worlds. It worked for only so long as I ran out of scenarios for the dust mite family. Once again, I waded in and out of a state of derealization as my natural body chemistry, predisposed to panic disorder, won over the fabricated contemplation of Pamela's pampered feet. My next ploy was to think about sex with Pamela. It was out of the question. She was motionless, didn't make a sound, her head turned to the side watching the bright illumination from the bedside digital clock as I moved in and out of her.

The unsuccessful fantasies gave way to heavy breathing and morbid thoughts that didn't let up until I passed Buckeye, a town on the fringe of the western Phoenix metropolitan area.

The last half of the drive had taken its toll and any remnants of the Xanax had lost its edge. My hands were visibly trembling as the obsession of going crazy subsided when I neared civilization. Visibly physical symptoms such as the shakes were common at the end of prolonged attacks. Like my body was exorcising all the bottled up negativity. It was an exhausting existence.

Life Unbothered
Charlie Elliott

By the time I arrived in the city of Scottsdale, my stomach rumbled with hunger. I contemplated a stop at Denny's on Indian Bend Road just a few traffic lights from home. But as I drove by the restaurant, my car kept going. Just that fast I was scared of having a panic attack, even at my favorite casual restaurant. The drive, along with the flight the night before, quickly rejuvenated an expanding list of fears, some I hadn't experienced in years.

From past episodes, I knew how this mental process worked. Not just Denny's, but I would soon fear all restaurants and avoid them completely. Then supermarkets, then movie theaters, then a certain street, then getting stuck in traffic, even a certain song on the radio could trigger memories of a panic attack. The cycle was unstoppable once it gained momentum.

Pulling into my driveway with too much speed, my car skidded on the slick garage floor and almost hit an interior wall of the house. I poked my finger on the garage door remote with overkill just as my body lurched back into the seat after the hard stop. The door started its downward motion, closing me in, tucking me away from the outside world.

"Shit!" I yelled while getting out of the car. The garage door was almost all the way down, creating enough noise to drown out my voice from the neighbors.

"I can't take this anymore!" I announced as if I were shouting to others in the garage. My rage could only exert itself in expletives shouted to no one within the confines of my empty living space. The car was still running as I bowed my head and leaned against the warm hood. My mental state felt like it was becoming too much for me to overcome, even with my impending move.

The car engine purred at an idle seven hundred RPMs as the exhaust built up quickly in the enclosed two-car garage. My eyes started to burn ever so slightly. Maybe carbon monoxide was a convenient exit strategy, a better method than putting a gun to my head.

As the garage started smelling like some ill-ventilated bus depot, I momentarily recollected on life, why I felt this way when I didn't really have it that bad in a growing-up perspective. Still, numbness embodied me as the personal reflections flashed through, and though I wanted to embrace the noxious exhaust, the tinge of hesitation enacted a self-starting physical motion that substantiated I didn't have the guts to keep the car running. Choosing for that instant to kill the car engine instead of my brain cells, I stuck my arm through the open driver's side window and twisted the key. The car ceased spewing its waste. Weakened from the panic attacks and possibly the car exhaust, I walked into the house and fell to the floor. I rolled over on my side and balled up into a fetal position on the carpet. My eyes closed and I immediately began to dream about being on an airplane, soaring away to some exotic destination without the burdensome luggage of panic attacks.

10. It's About the Sex

Just as the plane broke through the overcast in my dream and I soared above white puffy clouds, my cell phone rang. Uncurling from my sleeping fetal position, I removed the phone from my pocket.

"Hello?" a feeble shriek came from my dry vocal chords.

"Hi. It's me," the voice said.

I cleared my throat. "Who?"

"Me."

Silence.

"PA-MEL-A," she elongated her name, which assisted in jogging my memory.

"Oh… hi, Pamela."

"Who'd ya think it was?"

"I don't know. I'm sorry, I just—"

"Are you with another girl right now?" Pamela snorted.

"What? No."

"You still driving?"

"No. I just got home a little while ago." I expected her to speak, but a pause ensued.

"You hung up on me a couple of hours ago, Pamela. Why are you calling me back?"

"I hung up because you were being an asshole. But now I'm calling to see if you want to come down to my apartment. You haven't seen it yet."

"No, uh… I don't feel good right now."

"You don't want to come over?" Pamela asked, her voice acquiring a touch of an angry tone, the one she commonly articulated before the impending crescendo.

"Why don't you come up here instead?" I offered.

"No way, Wade. You'll just try to get me in bed. I want you to come down here."

"Sorry, I can't do it right now."

"Do you have another girlfriend already or something?"

"No, of course not. I just got home from California and don't feel like driving anymore. Also, I don't feel that great."

"I don't see why you won't come to my apartment. Are you having those dizzy-headed problems again?"

"No," I answered quickly.

"You're such an asshole, Wade. I'm trying to be nice."

"Pamela, I just don't feel well enough to drive to your apartment right this moment, that's all. It doesn't have to do with anything else."

"Well, I was just trying to see if we could try and work our relationship out. Of course, you'd have to decline that new job you got and get one here first before we could get back together."

"Get back together?"

"I've put a lot of time in you and I just turned twenty-four. It's my time to have a good life with nice things. You want me to throw that all away?"

A good life…nice things. Things were important to Pamela, or rather the appearance of nondescript material stuff. Marriage wasn't a question of happiness; it was an affirmation of affluent normalcy.

"Pamela, would you want to be with me if I had no money?" I asked.

Pamela hesitated, and I had the distinct feeling she was contorting her face.

"Well, I think you still have money, so I wouldn't know. You'll probably always have money, and after what I've put up from you, I deserve to live a life like all those rich bitches who used to bring their fancy cars down to your shop for cleaning."

"You know, you were so much nicer at the beginning of our relationship," I said.

"What the fuck do you expect? I was going to get married and you decided not to. I can't believe I even called tonight. I can't believe I was going to marry you. You're useless, you know that?"

"I'm beginning to figure that out."

"I can't believe you don't care about throwing away our relationship. If you don't want to come over, then I'm going to move too. Probably back to Michigan."

"You do that, Pamela."

Pamela snorted into the receiver. "Oh fuck you! You don't even care."

"It's not that, Pamela, it's—"

"I'm going to move. Since I have to pay rent now, you owe me some money and I'll need some cash to leave your sorry ass and this state."

When I was about to ask Pamela about how much money she needed, the doorbell chimed two loud rings. I stumbled to the front door with the phone in my hand. I pushed my eye against the peephole and saw my neighbor Colleen on the other side. Despite the skewed proportion from the curvature of the eyehole, she looked as good as ever. I scanned the stunning full-length black sequin dress she was wearing before drawing my face away from the front door.

"Uh, Pamela, the movers are here to give me a quote, so I've got to go."

"Movers? Fucking movers? It's eight o'clock at night, what kind of movers work at this time?"

"Very diligent and nice ones," I answered.

"So you're really going. Forget about the money you owe me, I'll just pawn the ring. Have a nice life, shithead."

Click.

When my phone screen went blank and Pamela's name disappeared, I dropped it on the kitchen counter and went to greet Colleen at the front door.

"Got your message," she said. "I just returned from a charity benefit."

"Wow, you look great," I said, once again eyeing her black sequin dress.

"You always say that. I could be strangling you and you'd say I looked great."

"No… that's when you'd look breathtaking."

She nodded her head. "Good choice of words. Where've you been?"

"In Los Angeles."

"Well, I got your mail while you were gone. It started sticking out of the mailbox."

"Thanks. Sorry, I forgot to tell you I was going."

She moved her face closer to mine. "I see your cheek isn't red anymore."

"Fortunately, Pamela throws like a girl."

Colleen smiled as we gave each other a lighthearted ogle before she glanced past me and saw a portion of the empty living room. "So Pamela's all gone?"

I looked behind me at the disencumbered space. "Oh yeah."

She cocked her head and flashed me a cute grin. "You look tired. Why don't you come over for some vodka gimlets?"

"That would be breathtaking," I said. "Let me just change my shirt first. I'll meet you over there."

I entered Colleen's house without knocking and sat on a puffy couch in her living room while she made our drinks. Her home décor was typical middle-aged divorced chic—truckloads of furniture way too nice for the modest house.

"I'm glad you came back when you did," Colleen said as she handed me a tall frosted cocktail glass. "I'm going to Nevada tomorrow for two weeks. My mother is having a cholecystectomy."

"Is that some kind of religious experience?"

"I wish. She's having her gallbladder removed. Pardon my vernacular, I was a nurse while you were still in diapers."

I stared off at her vast array of decorative furniture and became a little melancholy. This was the last time I would be able to see Colleen.

"Well, I'm going somewhere too," I said. "I'm moving to California next week."

"You're moving next week?"

"Yeah. Sorry for the short notice, but I took a job over there."

Colleen sat next to me on the couch and rubbed her eyes. "Oh… I'm happy and sad at the same time. I'm glad for you, though. You need a change."

"But I'm going to really miss you."

Colleen kissed my cheek. "You know, we couldn't have kept this up forever. We've been able to have a very chemically charged relationship without screwing it up with emotions. But until Pamela left, I thought you were getting married."

"What do you think would've happened to us then?" I asked.

"I don't know, we never discussed it. I had planned to stop fooling around after you got married. What were you going to do, just continue having sex with the *other* woman?"

"I've thought about it, but you're just so damn sexy that I would've had a hard time letting you go."

"I know. I feel the same way. But maybe this is a good thing. I was so happy when you didn't get married, but then felt sel because I knew we couldn't go on forever."

"I think the best thing to do is just enjoy the time we have left."

Colleen stroked my leg, moving her hand to my crotch. "God, you get me going."

She rose from the couch and walked into her bedroom. I put my hands behind my head and sat back as our relationship went through my mind. We never broached any deeply emotional issues while Pamela was still around. Our limited time together was mostly about the desirous sex and harmless conversation. Despite her age compared to mine, which never bothered me at all, Colleen was like a partner in an escaped way where we could enjoy all the intimacies without the daily burdens of reality.

Colleen returned after she shed her black cocktail dress. A sheer pink silk robe replaced the sparkly outfit. In dramatic fashion, she walked in front of me with her arms extended.

"You like?"

"Looks great."

I arose from the couch and stood next to Colleen, slid my right hand through the front of the robe, and gently nestled my fingers between her legs. She bent her knees outward slightly and let me stroke across her. I tipped my head down and kissed her neck as Colleen moaned softly.

"If you keep this up, my legs are going to collapse," she whispered.

She gently pushed me into her bedroom and we fell on the bed in a dramatically bouncy fashion. I rolled on my side to turn the bedside lamp on. She liked sex with the lights on, and so did I.

Colleen opened her robe, the sides pressed flat on the sheets. I kissed both of her firm breasts before working down the center of her torso with my lips, not stopping until I was between her opened legs. After four minutes, Colleen's body shook as her thighs clamped tightly around my head. For a few seconds I was deaf and suffocating—the headlock was pure bliss—breathtaking in an exhilarating way, not the usual reaction to the lack of breath due to panic. When her legs popped back open, I lifted my head and moved to her side while she recovered from her orgasm.

"Oh, you are *too* good," Colleen said as she rolled over on her side to face me.

"The pleasure is entirely mine."

"The bottom half of my body is still tingling." She kissed my wet lips before sitting up and swinging her legs over the side of the bed. "Let me get your drink." An overacted sigh blew from her mouth. "I'm such an impolite hostess; didn't even bring your drink in for you *before* we had sex. And take all your clothes off. Stay a while."

I disrobed and placed my clothes on a large bedroom chair covered with swirling gilded upholstery. Colleen returned with my drink and a cocktail napkin. She placed them on the nightstand.

"Here you are, Mr. Hampton," she said. "By the time you finish this drink, I'll be ready for round two."

I jumped back on the bed, gulped down the entire drink, and slammed the empty glass down on the napkin.

"Round two coming up," I said. "I love your tenacity."

Colleen had a seductive look on her face as she got on top of me and straddled my body. At forty-nine years old, she could be on top and still look terrific. A naked sensual older woman was a vision of beauty to me. Watching her from below with my hands firmly positioned on the soft skin of her midriff was pure joy. The ills of my drive through the desert whittled to nothing, replaced with the flow of temporary ecstasy. The drive never happened, there was no airplane ride, the panic attacks never occurred, the garage was never filled with exhaust and I wasn't even in California earlier. Colleen was my Xanax as I watched her body drift up and down. There were no problems from within as my body pressed and released against the mattress.

* * * *

I woke up the next morning as Colleen placed a glass of orange juice by the side of the bed. Our nude bodies were sticky from the sex the night before.

"I've never had you for the whole night. It's nice," she said.

"I've never seen you in the morning. You look ravishing."

"Not breathtaking?" She smiled as I sat up and took two large gulps of the pulpy orange juice. Colleen stretched out on the bed beside me, her head resting on her hand.

"So what are you going to do in California?" she asked.

"Going to work for a friend."

"You know, I think it's great you're moving, I really do. You haven't been the same since you shut down your business. How long has it been since you closed it?"

"Just over two months."

"Why did you shut the business down anyway? I remember when you'd clean my car, the place always looked busy."

I nudged next to her and recited the answer I had rehearsed in my head so a cohesive response would always be ready whenever someone asked. "Basically, the business didn't fulfill my expectations. It wasn't a total financial failure, but after running the thing day-to-day for over three years, I got kind of burnt out."

Colleen kissed my forehead. "Why didn't you sell the business?" she asked.

"It was easier just to shut it down and sell the equipment. The business was debt-free, so it was an uncomplicated deal."

"No debt? How'd you get the money to start it up?"

I gulped down the last of my orange juice. "The proceeds from stock gifted to me by my parents when I was younger. Originally, it was to help cover college expenses, but over the years, the stock gains were large enough to pay for college. Actually, with the gains and reinvestments, I could've gone to graduate school or even medical school and paid for it. But no, I wanted to own a business."

"I'm sorry your business didn't work out the way you hoped. But you've been very successful with me."

"I have? Are you telling me the sex is good?"

Colleen rolled on her back and stared at the ceiling for a moment.

"I know you probably think our relationship is just sexual, but it's more than that. I'm sure you've had plenty of girls flocking around you over the years. But underneath that beautiful skin of yours is a complex man. That's the attraction for me—the sex is a fantastic bonus. And you know—I *do* love you."

I shot upright. "You love me?"

Colleen let out a deep laugh. She shifted her eyes over to me, breaking her stare at the ceiling. "Don't get paranoid. I'm not talking in the 'let's live together and get engaged' way. Hell, I'm over twenty years older than you. All I'm trying to say is when you come over, we get naked so fast there's not enough time to really talk. I want you to know how much you've meant to me. I'm not just some Mrs. Robinson."

"Well if you were, at least let me have a crack at your daughter."

She leaned over and whispered slowly, "Even if I had a daughter, I'd still turn you on more than her."

"You probably got that right."

"I'm going to have to pack and be out of here in a couple of hours to leave for Nevada. I just wanted to tell you that our friendship has helped me through a rough time. You basically kept me from losing it after my divorce." Tears welled in Colleen's eyes. "I was so lonely, though my husband and I hadn't had a relationship for years."

I kissed a tear that fell on her left cheek. "And you helped me through my engagement," I said. "So we're even."

Colleen rolled on top of me and wedged her arms around my body. We kissed feverishly for a minute before she rested her head on my chest.

"No, I'm not going to cry," she said. "I have to remember I was going to cut you off after you got married anyway. So I'll treat your moving like the wedding."

"Well, I'm not getting married, but whatever works for you…"

"Oh, you've already done your work. Look, I'm almost fifty, and I feel better than I ever have. I feel sexier, more confident—and you are a big part of that."

"Wow, I didn't know that. So what's your sexy body going to do without me?"

"Probably be stuck with old men. I guess I'll have to settle for that."

"Don't cause too many heart attacks."

She pulled her arms out from under me and arose from the bed. She sauntered to her dresser and retrieved a pair of red silk panties from the top drawer.

"Something to remember me by," she said, then dropped the panties on my chest. "Take them to California with you."

"I'll put them next to me at night and dream about you."

Colleen returned to the bed. "That's cute. But let me give you some advice since I'm an older, wiser woman. When you find that special person, within an acceptable age range of course, open up to her and let your heart go. That's when you'll reach the glory of absolute happiness."

"Wait a minute. I think that was too deep for me. I'm not sure if I got that."

"You'll understand someday," Colleen said. She sighed, then gave me a wry smile. "There is *one* thing I need you to do before I go." She pushed my head toward her waist and wiggled her legs.

"You want me to do it again, Mrs. Robinson?"

"I'd love you to, Benjamin."

11. For Something a Little Different

Over the next couple of days, I called a realtor to list the house, got the movers set up to take my stuff over to California, took care of my mail and online bills, and threw unwanted items away. All the while, I couldn't shake one nagging task from my mind. The Xanax wasn't working as well as I wanted it to after taking it per prescription since the morning I woke up in Colleen's bed. Being terrified of experiencing panic attacks during the drive back to move to Los Angeles, I thought a companion could possibly help me get through the ride. At least if I did go crazy during the trek, somebody could drive the car to safety.

Through a couple of sketchy references from licensed and unlicensed sources, I came upon a guy named Wink, or Dr. Travel as he called himself professionally. Dr. Travel apparently provided a turnkey logistic operation for those who had limited travel ability—physical or mental, it didn't matter to him. When I reached him by phone, the ruckus on the other end of the line sounded like he was at an early afternoon keg party. It was hard to hear him above the country music in the background.

"I need to get to Los Angeles," I said.

"What?" It sounded like he pulled the phone away from his mouth, and in a barely audible voice I heard, "Beautiful, baby. Here's a five for you."

"Wink?"

"Yeah, sorry about that. Call me Dr. Travel. So where do you need to go?"

"Los Angeles."

"Flying or driving."

"Driving."

As the country song continued in the background, I heard Wink say in a muffled voice, "Yes, I love cowgirls—here's another five." There was a subtle rubbing noise for a few seconds before he put his mouth back to the phone. "Sorry about that, just getting some work done."

"Can you get me to L.A?"

"Yeah, no problem. Driving to L.A. You got the car?"

"Yes, I need to get my car over there too."

The conversation paused once more as I heard him utter something. The only two words I caught were "table" and "dance."

"Okay… What's your name again?" Wink asked.

"Wade Hampton."

"Okay, Wade. What's your condition?"

"My condition?"

"Why do you need me to get you to L.A? Are you in a wheelchair or something?"

"No, I'm, uh, agoraphobic."

"Yeah? Perfect. I got just the medication package for you. I'll get you to Cali with no stress or fear. This isn't my first rodeo for that one." Sounds muffled again as his phone must have moved from his ear. "Not you, baby," he said. "You're my *first* rodeo."

"Wink, I mean, Dr. Travel, I would like to leave this Thursday, in three days. Do you have availability?"

"Yes, yes, yes! Oh yeah."

"So you can do it?"

"What?" Wink asked. "Oh, you said this Thursday? Let me check."

I listened to the remainder of the country song playing in the background, which was followed by AC/DC's "Highway to Hell." Appropriate song for the situation.

"Thursday will do," Wink said. "It's three hundred bucks an hour plus expenses. I'll also need a return plane ticket, preferably from LAX, on Thursday night."

"Okay, I can do that."

"Great. Give me your address and I'll be there at nine in the morning on Thursday, give or take a few. I'll have to get an Uber friend to drive me over."

It sounded like he was grunting in pain while I gave him my information. I imagined him writing it down somewhere, perhaps on the tits of his exotic cowgirl dancer.

"So I'll see you at nine this Thursday?" I asked.

"Ohhhhh, yes darling. Yes!"

I didn't think that was a confirmation of our appointment, but I assumed he got all the information he could handle at the moment.

I stared at the phone for a couple of seconds after I hung up. It amazed me that someone could actually have a large enough clientele to make a living by moving invalids while charging $300 an hour, plus expenses. But if Wink could spend his afternoons sitting in strip joints shoveling bills to dancers, then he must have been doing something right.

Putting Dr. Travel out of my mind, I looked at my to-do list and saw there was only one more call I needed to make. I dialed Cameron Engernald's office number. Cameron was an insurance agent about my age who handled *all my business and health insurance needs*. At least that's the way she described it. My last attempt to reach her was when I was looking for a date while driving back from Los Angeles the week before. I was calling to cancel my health insurance because it was an overpriced policy with very little benefits.

"This is Cameron Engernald."

"Hi Cameron, Wade Hampton here."

"Wade Hampton," she said my name slowly. "What's up? Started another business and need a quote?"

Before I answered, I noticed how officiously sexy her voice always sounded.

"Uh, no Cameron. Actually, I want to cancel my health insurance."

"What? Cancel it? Did someone give you a better price, because if they did—"

"No, nobody's cutting your throat. I'm moving to California and just don't want to pay that much for a single policy, so I'm going to forego insurance for a while."

"Why? You can keep your policy even if you're moving. And besides, you'll be hit with the lack of coverage tax penalty."

"I don't care," I said with zero emotion in my voice, or my soul.

"When are you moving?"

"On Thursday."

"This Thursday?"

"Yeah."

"Just because you're moving doesn't mean you have to cancel your policy. Why don't you call me after you move and we can adjust it?"

"I'd rather just get rid of it for now, Cameron."

There was a short pause. I heard Cameron ticking her keyboard before she broke the silence.

"Hey Wade, let's play golf tomorrow. We haven't done that for a while. We used to play a lot before you started living with… Pamela."

"Yeah, I know," I muttered.

"How's that *thing* doing?"

"We broke up," I said casually. "Hey, I don't know if I can make it for golf tomorrow. Why don't you come over tonight? We can talk about the policy."

"Can't do it. I've got a training seminar to go to."

"Blow it off. Those things are usually boring anyway."

"No, I can't. But let's play golf tomorrow. I've got a tee time at TPC for eleven. I was going to play with a couple of potential clients, but they backed out. It'll give me time to talk you out of canceling your insurance with me."

"Tomorrow? Isn't Tuesday ladies day or something?"

"No, they don't have that anymore. Reverse sexual discrimination, you know. So you won't get kicked off the course by angry men-haters."

I thought about it for a moment, and realized I had taken care of all the moving details and did have time to play golf—and the unexpected possibility arose that I may be able to snuggle next to Cameron one more time.

"Okay, I'll play. But I still want you to cancel the policy."

"Great. I'll meet you at TPC tomorrow at eleven. I won't do anything with your insurance until after the game. At least give me that."

12. Golfing with the Enemy

Upon awakening the next morning at nine o'clock, I took my morning dose of Xanax, shaved, and jumped in the shower. In my current state, anxiety would be bringing me to a status of pre-panic as I would obsess about leaving the house. The fact that I had never experienced an authentic panic attack on a golf course was one of the few comforts that afforded me.

Cameron and I used to play golf together almost weekly until Pamela moved in. In college, she was a member of the Arizona State University golf team until a wrist injury ended her competitive career. Her skills hadn't diminished much over the years. She still carried a three handicap. Off the golf course, our relationship was laced with casual athletic sex. Cameron was a driven woman, the kind who would screw around with no need for emotional attachment—as long as it served her purposes. That was her endearing quality.

I ironed my golf outfit, socks and underwear included, which took an hour to get the clothes just right. I rounded up my golf bag and hit the button on the garage wall to engage the door opener. The air rushing into the garage revealed a beautiful spring morning. Crisp, clean eighty-degree air swirled around me as I put my clubs in the trunk.

At twenty minutes before eleven o'clock, I exited my driveway. It was a short drive to the TPC of Scottsdale, the course that hosts the Phoenix Open, a PGA tournament held every year in January or early February. Though a corporate sponsor had attached its name to the tournament as with most professional golf venues, I sided with the old timers and still referred to it as the Phoenix Open.

Although I hadn't played much golf since the engagement to Pamela, the one thing I still loved about living in Scottsdale was the accessibility to some great golf courses. The Phoenix area boasted over two hundred courses within an hour's drive. Many of the nicer courses in the area catered to people visiting from the North and Midwest to escape the harsher winter climates. The snowbirds flocked by the thousands to the milder temperatures the Sonoran desert offered during the winter and early spring.

I changed into my spiked golf shoes in the TPC parking lot and toted my clubs to the rack in front of a row of golf carts. A climb up a short flight of stairs lined with purple pansies brought me into the pro shop.

"You're on the tee in five minutes," the aspiring young golf pro working behind the counter said. "Put your clubs on cart number twenty-seven. Ms. Engernald's clubs are already on the cart."

"Are there just the two of us?" I asked.

The guy looked down at the starter sheet. "No, you're playing with a gentleman named Mr. Michaels. He's from out of town."

As I walked back down the steps outside the pro shop, a familiar voice called out.

"Hey, Wade."

Life Unbothered — Charlie Elliott

I saw Cameron Engernald in her pressed golf skirt and red sleeveless top. She was slender and tall, about five feet ten. She had her blonde hair pulled back in a short ponytail. From the back, she could've been the prototype model used for a Barbie doll. But in close proximity, her face had a rough look to it and her frizzled hair teemed with split ends. The complete close-up package would be more appropriate for the "Unwholesome Barbie" model.

"Hi Cameron," I said.

"I was wondering where you were. Didn't see you out on the range."

"Didn't make it to the range this morning."

"Going out cold, huh?" She laughed nervously as I hugged her. We hadn't been together for a long enough time to feel immediately comfortable. "How many strokes do you want for that?"

"No strokes, that's okay. I haven't even held a club for a couple of months."

"Excuses will get you nowhere, Wade. But I'll play from the blue tees with you."

I strapped my clubs on the passenger side of the cart. Cameron always drove the cart. It was a control thing. I inspected Cameron's tan legs as she bent over to retie one of her golf shoes. She looked up and caught me staring. Taking it in stride, she smiled.

"So, you broke up with Pamela."

"Yeah. I had enough of her and called off the wedding plans."

"I'll tell you what, I almost beat the shit out of that bitch the last time I saw her."

"I know," I said, then followed my words with a laugh. "Jamie Holitzer's party. When was that, about seven months ago?"

"Uh-huh. She threw a drink on me for some reason. If you hadn't gotten her out of there, I would've killed her. I guess that was also the last time I saw you."

"It was."

"Next on the tee is the Engernald, Hampton, Michaels, threesome."

Cameron looked at the speaker that announced our names. "Come on, let's go to the tee."

We drove to the first hole as the foursome of tourists playing in front of us finished their tee shots. A man in checkered slacks dribbled his drive through the desert brush before the ball skidded its way to the first cut of fairway grass.

"May be a long day for him," a squat round man in the cart next to us said. "I'm Maury Michaels. My wife was going to join us, but she decided to go shopping. So it's just us three."

Cameron extended her arm to him while I went to the back of the cart to retrieve my golf glove. "I'm Cameron," she said, then pointed to me, "and that is Wade."

"What a pretty couple," Maury noted as he glanced at both of us. "Are you married?"

I slipped the glove on my left hand. "No, but we've slept together on many occasions. That was before I got engaged."

Maury's face pursed as if someone had slapped a wet towel across his cheek. After my answer registered in his head, he belted out a boisterous laugh.

"Are all you Arizonians this funny?"

"No," Cameron answered. "Wade is about as funny as it gets—at least in Scottsdale."

As we waited for the foursome in front of us to clear the fairway, Maury told us he was visiting from Canton, Ohio to scout for a residence when he retired in the next couple of years.

When the group ahead moved to the green, I volunteered to hit my tee shot first. From the blue tees, the hole was a short par four, three hundred sixty-six yards. The wise choice was a long iron, but I foolishly chose the driver, trying to put my ball past the wash that would leave a short approach to the green. End result: I yanked a shot left of the fairway and luckily caught the fluffy rough about two yards shy of the desert waste and prickly cacti. Cameron then stepped on the tee and placed her shot perfectly in the middle of the fairway about ten yards in front of the wash. Maury's shoulders tightened a bit when he saw Cameron's shot—adding to the stress was the fact that she didn't use the ladies tee.

The next few holes were challenging, but I managed to avoid making a fool out of myself. My timing was a little rusty. The finesse shots such as chipping and putting were out of sync, but I wasn't concerned with the way I was playing. It was nice to get out in the fresh air and scenery… and the possibility of being next to a woman after the round. Maury seemed to settle down and relax after getting over the initial intimidation of playing with two low handicappers. Between shots, he would ask me questions about the Phoenix area.

"Where's the best place to stay in town?" Maury asked.

"Where are you staying now?"

"Camelback Inn."

"Yeah, Camelback is a nice older resort. But the next time you come out, try The Boulders. It's always been run with class."

Maury proceeded to ask me questions about housing developments, restaurants, and golf courses around the area.

"You're like a one-man fucking chamber of commerce," Cameron commented as I informed Maury about the area.

After our tee shots on the eighth hole, Cameron got down to business as we carted along the edge of the fairway.

"Hey Wade, I want to talk to you about your insurance," she said.

"I think I'm going to cancel it."

"You don't want to be without insurance. What happens if you have a medical problem?"

"That policy doesn't even pay for my medical expenses. The last four times I visited a doctor, the insurance paid nothing. I still have the stack of mail they sent me that probably cost more than the stupid visits."

"The insurance should pay," Cameron insisted, "unless you're seeing a bunch of shrinks or something."

I glanced at her and tried to suppress a reaction. "Just cancel the policy, Cameron. Hell, if you did personal auto insurance, I'd transfer that over to you. But I don't want to pay for medical."

"So, your car is more important than your body?"

I looked to the sloping green about eighty yards ahead and thought about it. *Right now it is.*

Cameron scooted closer to me on the vinyl seat and creased her eyebrows together. "You know what? I brought you out here and played golf with you to save one little health policy. You used to be a great customer of mine when you had all those insured employees at your company, now you're down to one policy. You know how that affects me?"

Maury pulled his cart to the side of ours. I glanced at him and smiled, trying to diffuse the tension created by Cameron's raised voice.

"Yeah Cameron, I noticed that we haven't played golf for a while," I said.

She sighed hard as she jammed the pedal down on the cart, leaving Maury behind to hit his next shot. She didn't speak again until we were standing on the green watching Maury line up a particularly slippery downhill putt.

"Business is business, Wade. If I can't make money, there's no use doing it. I've got big plans and goals I'm trying to meet—just like it seemed you used to."

Cameron's mood cooled for the next few holes as she simmered down. I had forgotten how hot her temper was; she could be giggling one moment and ripping out your eyeballs the next. Luckily, most of her outbursts were short-lived.

The round sped up on the back nine as the tourist foursome in front of us quit playing. They must have had enough of the dry air and the beautiful contrasting scenery of green and brown—or their ill-matching plaid outfits were suddenly deemed unfit to be worn on the course. A birdie on the fourteenth hole lifted Cameron's spirits. It brought her to three over par and two strokes ahead of me. After she executed a perfect tee shot on the next hole, I saw an opportunity to make a move.

"You know, Cameron, I've been thinking about what you said. I'm not quite sold on keeping the insurance, but I'm considering it. Let's talk about it more tonight at my house."

"Tonight? I'm not going to be with you tonight." I could see the wheels turning in her mind as she realized what I was asking. "Is that why you called? To get a piece of ass?"

"That's not exactly why I called, but it would be nice."

"You asshole!" she shouted.

From across the fairway, I saw Maury's head jerk up and look our way as he scouted for his errant ball.

"I know we used to be fuck-buddies," Cameron continued, "but I'm a professional now."

"A professional fuck-buddy?" I asked.

"No, a professional businessperson, you dick. And I'm not going to go out and screw you for the night. Those days are gone."

I put my left arm around her as she drove the cart. "You know, it used to be so much more fun when we played golf."

"Fuck you!"

The remainder of the round—complete silence with the exception of calling out my score after each hole. When we walked off the eighteenth green, Maury Michaels seemed amused by our somewhat volatile company, but relieved it was the last hole. Cameron walked to the cart while I said goodbye to Maury.

"Sorry about all the commotion. Cameron and I have a fiery past."

Maury smiled. "Well, you still make a pretty couple."

On the drive back to the clubhouse from the eighteenth green, Cameron handed me the scorecard.

"You shot a seventy-nine. I beat you by four strokes," she said.

I stared blankly at the card. "Then I guess I owe you a drink."

"You don't owe me anything, except maybe an apology."

"I'm sorry," I said.

"Not good enough."

We stopped in front of the clubhouse and lifted our clubs off the back of the cart. Without saying anything, Cameron started walking to the parking lot.

"Cameron," I called from behind her. "Wait."

She stopped and turned around.

"Come over to my house for just an hour," I pleaded.

"You want me to come over because you're probably lonely and on the rebound. I'm not going to replace that bitch just so you can shoot your load. You know, things are different. I have a career. I'm successful. I now eat guys like you for lunch."

"Well, I've eaten you for breakfast, lunch, dinner, a midnight snack, high tea, happy hour, and even on Bastille Day. So what's your point, Cameron?"

"My point is I'm not the easy girl you used to have under your spell. Go to California and find some new victims, you asshole."

"I'm just asking you to come over and talk."

Her lips became toothpick thin as she shifted her eyes away from me. "You know what? I'm going to cancel your menial insurance policy. And now that we're not doing business together, there's no reason to talk again."

"Cameron, I never knew our relationship was based on me doing business with you. That's pretty screwed up."

Cameron looked at me, spread her arms apart in surrender, and beamed a sarcastic smile. "Well, Wade, welcome to the wonderful world of commission sales."

Visions of Cameron's body wrapped around mine filled the time on the short ride home from the golf course. I was bummed that the two of us weren't on our way to getting naked. The distress made me yearn for a woman to wash away the impending mental troubles I knew would engulf me if I went home and sat idle.

In complete desperation, I almost went to a local Asian fusion restaurant where a girl I knew worked, but there was that lava lamp sensation, my head warping and skewing the perception of my surroundings. The usual trigger systems ensued—heart pounding, breath gulping, lungs clamping. There was no way I was going to make the ten-mile drive to the restaurant on the small chance I could find her, or even be with her. Instead of a diverted drive, I kept the car guided in home's direction. My body was telling me it was time to return to my self-imposed incarceration and loneliness.

13. The Slumber Party

My shoes clacked on the tile in the front entryway of my empty house as I approached the door to meet Wink, or Dr. Travel as he insisted over the phone. As the door opened, I realized why his mother named him Wink. He bore a stunning resemblance to Wink Martindale of old game show fame. He had the same jutting full-tooth smile and slick hair as the emcee. Wink, to my surprise, was punctual.

"I'm Dr. Travel," he said, smiling with both rows of teeth. "You ready to go?"

"Yeah, I'm ready. How exactly does this work?" I asked.

Wink entered the house and placed his old leather tote on the tile floor. "It's real simple. I have a mixture of medication—pharmaceutical and natural—that you'll take. By the time we leave Phoenix city limits, you'll be completely out for at least a few hours. You shouldn't experience any agoraphobia while on the medication." He smiled again and directed his attention to the front door. "Hey is that your BMW out there?"

"Yes. It's what you are driving to Los Angeles."

"Cool. Those chrome rims are smokin."

Looking at Wink, 'cool' and 'smokin' were not words I would have expected to come out of his mouth. He was about forty years old, short, and dressed in a Hawaiian shirt and baggy walking shorts. His white socks covered his legs below the knees. Strip joint dweeb was the look that came to mind.

"I'm kind of nervous about taking some pills, what are they?"

Wink smiled, again, and opened his leather bag. "That's a professional secret."

"Well, I guess if you're a doctor, you know what you are doing."

He lifted his finger as if to make a point and pulled out a tiny clear bag of pills. "Well... I'm not actually a doctor, the law permits me to say I'm a counselor." He tapped the small bag of pills against his palm. "But I do have killer access to some drugs."

'Killer' was another word I didn't expect in his vocabulary.

I was already petrified about the drive before I actually met Dr. Travel in person. His demeanor didn't help ease the apprehension. I worried about where I would end up after I awakened from the drive. I imagined Wink dumping my drugged body at some run-down motel near the Mexican border and taking off with my car.

"I'm already on Xanax, so I don't know what else you need to give me."

Dr. Travel flashed his teeth. "Xanax will intermingle real well with these other drugs. That's perfect—it'll give you an extra kick. You ready?"

"I guess so," I mumbled.

I had no options left to get me back to California, except via the normal way of getting in the car myself and driving. It was pathetic that I had to surrender myself to a guy who calls himself Dr. Travel, but I was too mentally fatigued to argue. So I yielded to him. Wink handed me the bag of pills.

"Take all eight pills. Don't worry about what they are, but I certify that all medicine I prescribe is totally legal and pharmaceutical. Just pop them in your mouth."

I walked over to the kitchen sink and lowered my head to the faucet. I couldn't believe I was actually doing this, but I swallowed all eight in one gulp.

Wink smiled once more as the pills tumbled down my esophagus. "Okay, so let me go over the billing, but first, you got my plane ticket?" he asked.

I walked to my packed duffle bag and fetched the pre-assigned boarding pass along with a printout of the route. "Yeah. You're arriving back here this evening. Here's the map also."

"Perfect. Okay, the trip is three hundred dollars an hour. I'm not responsible for any traffic delays, accidents, or any problems, physical or mental, that might occur during our time together or afterward. You are responsible for any gas, food, and other supplies we may need. The medication you just took, that's on me. No charge." He pulled a wrinkled piece of paper from his bag. "Sign at the bottom and the fun starts. Any questions?"

I was wondering why he waited to go over the contractual details until after I had taken the pills. "No questions," is all I could say as I scribbled someone's signature on the paper.

"Great. I just need five hundred up front and we'll be on our way."

Then I realized why he waited to talk business until after I took the pills. I opened my wallet and handed him five bills.

As Wink maneuvered my car through the Phoenix traffic in silence, I gradually floated away from reality, my brain wrapped in paralyzed incontinence. My neck gave way as my head melted against the curvature of the side window, my body blobbed into the fine hand-stitched leather seat. There was no impending desert or isolated land. I would not be watching the exits on the interstate for a place to turn around. There would be no panic attacks. By the time we entered the city of Glendale just west of Phoenix, the last thing I saw was a big warping Taco Bell sign, and then I think I saw God eating a Burrito Supreme. My eyes closed and I was in the full and competent care of Dr. Travel.

* * * *

"How do you feel?" Dr. Stanley Crouch asked, twisting the left tip of his bushy mustache with his fingers.

"I feel fine," I answered.

The truth was I still had a hangover from Dr. Travel's drug stash the day before. I had to give Wink credit though, he did get me to Los Angeles with no panic episodes. I awakened from his drug concoction as we merged onto the 105 freeway in the heart of L.A. We even had time before his flight to stop by one of the many strip joints in proximity to the airport. After spending a groggy hour with him around naked girls, I formed a clearer picture of what Wink was experiencing when I first spoke with him on the phone.

"So, anything new?" Dr. Crouch asked.

"I decided to take a job in San Pedro, so I moved back here yesterday. I'm starting next week."

"You moved back to the area?"

"Yeah. I decided to come back here and work for my friend."

"How did you return to Los Angeles?" Dr. Crouch prodded. "Did you fly?"

"No, I drove. I had to get my car here."

"No problems driving alone from Phoenix?"

"Nothing I can remember." I stammered a bit. "I had a guy from Arizona drive out with me."

"So you had someone with you," Dr. Crouch stated, scribbling on this notepad. "Did it help having someone with you?"

"It seemed to make a little difference."

Dr. Crouch sat in his leather chair and looked at me for a few seconds. I tried to stare him down, but my eyes darted to the floor.

"Wade, if I told you to drive up to San Francisco right now and spend the night at a hotel and drive back here tomorrow, would you do it? And," Dr. Crouch added, "I would pay for the trip. Would you do it?"

"Well, I have to start my new job soon—"

"No," he interrupted. "Let's say you didn't have to be at your job for a week—you were totally free of commitments. Would you take the drive by yourself?"

"I don't know if I would feel comfortable driving all the way up to San Francisco."

"How about if I paid you one million dollars to fly down to San Diego tonight. Would you take the flight?"

"Is that a million dollars net or taxable?" I asked.

Dr. Crouch dropped his shoulders a couple of inches. "A million dollars cash, non-taxable. Would you fly?"

"Well… I'd try to."

"You'd try? Try? For a million dollars, I'd hop on that plane in an instant. And a few years ago, so would you. There would be no trying, it would just be done. Why do you think you'd have to *try* when that is an easy, short flight?"

"Because I would be afraid of having a panic attack on the plane," I conceded.

"Exactly," Dr. Crouch agreed, leaning forward in his chair. "You see how much you're avoiding. I know you don't want to admit it, but do you really want to live your life this way?"

"No."

Dr. Crouch swiveled his chair around to retrieve two sheets of paper and a prescription pad from his old maple desk.

"I want to use a different class of drugs on you. They're called MAO inhibitors, or MAOIs. They're not widely prescribed anymore, but I'd like to see if they help."

"MAOIs, I've read about them. Those are for psychotics or something, aren't they?"

Dr. Crouch darted a look at me. "No, you're not a psychopath or anything of the sort. MAO inhibitors are known to help with depression and anxiety disorders. The particular drug I'm prescribing is called Nardil, it's been around for decades. There are some diet restrictions with this drug, so make sure you follow the guidelines." He handed me two sheets of instructions and I scanned the short list. "Do you have any problem with the diet restrictions?"

"No, I doubt it. I can eat like a dog, the same thing day after day."

"Good. Make sure you don't eat anything on that list, it's very important."

"What happens if I do?"

"Those foods have a high tyramine content which can cause very dangerous reactions such as sudden high blood pressure or stroke while on Nardil. That's one of the reasons why it's not prescribed much anymore."

"I really don't want to go on another drug. Isn't there anything else I can try besides medication?"

Dr. Crouch leaned over and put his elbows on his knees. "Do you know what mulch is?"

"You mean that wood stuff you put on the ground?"

"Exactly. It could be cedar, eucalyptus, cypress, pine or even synthetic."

"Okay, but what does this have to do with getting me better?"

"It's the symbolism of it," Dr. Crouch said as his eyes became softer in intensity. "Mulch can cover up imperfections in the ground. It can smooth out dips, can cover old dirt and leaves, it is a way of making the imperfect ground underneath look better. I want you to do an exercise where you feel like your body is, in essence, mulched. All the imperfections are gone on the outside and it will slowly transform you inside. It's a simple implement I use to help people defray their thoughts from external embarrassment. It helps keep your feelings in the present."

I looked around his office for a moment to reprocess the information. "Sounds a bit earthy to me."

"Just try it, Wade. You need the medication though. If the Nardil helps, we'll gradually reduce the Xanax dosage later."

"That would be okay with me. I worry about that stuff being addictive."

"Well, make sure you stay on the Xanax for now. I also want you to take one fifteen milligram pill of Nardil three times a day—morning, afternoon and evening," Dr. Crouch instructed.

"Another medication and some gardening advice," I whispered with skepticism as I exited his Beverly Hills office.

14. Employment

After an abridged search for living arrangements, I decided to rent an apartment at Capital Bluff, a condo-style complex on Capital Avenue in San Pedro. Capital Avenue was a four lane street that sloped its way down a hill eventually ending up at Gaffey Street, considered the old main road in the aged harbor town.

Capital Bluff was a gated apartment development with garaged parking and all the amenities expected in a pricey one-bedroom, eight hundred square-foot living space. My apartment fronted the often-busy Capital Avenue through an iron fence and a tall hedge of bushes planted for sound abatement.

The next day I arrived at Haverco just before eight o'clock in the morning. Richard Haverport's business was located at an obscure unnamed berth in the Los Angeles Harbor, or its flashier marketing name, Worldport L.A. Everyone just called it the Blue Berth due to a lone blue steel building on the facility. The company employed about forty union labor dockworkers under the veil of the ILWU, the longshoreman's union. According to Richard in an earlier phone conversation, I was the new director of administration for the rapidly growing company that provided heavy industrial maintenance and steel fabrication for the marine industry.

The Blue Berth was operated by the Harbor Department, the governmental authority of the Los Angeles Harbor. The Harbor Department owned two cranes at the berth used for container and cargo ship loading and unloading. To generate revenues, they leased the cranes to private carriers. Haverco also maintained the cranes to eliminate expensive downtime if the cranes failed in some way and delayed the loading or unloading process.

A Korean company leased the two gantry cranes at the Blue Berth. Their main business was buying scrap metal for pennies on the dollar locally and loading it on huge ships to send back to Korea. After a trek across the Pacific, the company would recycle the metals to transform the scrap into useable commodities such as automobiles and plates of steel to sell around the world.

The location was not a picturesque place. It was mostly a huge slab of concrete with some weeds poking out of large cracks in the pavement. Many locals considered the Los Angeles Harbor itself as a dirty, ugly area riddled with pollutants. While growing up on the hill above in Palos Verdes, I looked out over the Harbor every day and thought it a place of intrigue and beauty. The one hundred-twenty foot tall gantry cranes hovered high above the ground like huge praying insects, while container ships, giant moving islands of steel, lumbered their way in and out of the Harbor.

I walked into the large steel building that housed Haverco, passing by a couple of service trucks in the shop area. A lone door on the back wall led to a wide hallway where the offices were located. As I went through the door of Richard's office, he stood up and walked around his desk.

"Welcome to Haverco," Richard Haverport said, greeting me with a smile and hug.

"Are we going to hug every morning?" I asked.

"If you want to."

Richard walked behind his steel desk. Stacked piles of paper covered the desktop area around him. The office had the appearance of being decorated by a mechanic: neatly rolled blueprints leaned against the bare walls, large engineering and machinery parts books filled the bookshelves, the functional rubberized gray floor featured protruding bas-relief dots.

He chewed on his pen while studying a sheet of paper in front of him.

"Okay, Wade, I know we went over this a couple of days ago on the phone, but I need you to take care of most the administrative matters—hourly waged employee paychecks, worker's comp, health insurance, benefits, pensions, and all that other stuff I don't have time to do anymore."

Richard paused and I nodded to confirm my comprehension of the duties.

"But, what I need first is an updated safety manual. OSHA requires it and I couldn't show them an adequate current document on a visit they made last month. They gave me some time to get an updated manual put together. Think you can do that?"

"Yeah, I actually did one before for my business. Most of it can be boilerplate with the names changed, but we'll probably have to go into quite a bit more depth for safety procedures and injury reports since this is classified as dangerous work—at least from a liability standpoint."

"Good. Very good," Richard responded. "Okay, I've made some room for you in the next office. A new computer is on the desk. The other desk is for my secretary, but she's here only three days a week."

"No problem. I'll get started on the safety manual now if you want me to."

"Go ahead, I need a good one in two weeks. If you need anything—software, supplies, whatever, let me know."

"What should I wear to work?"

Richard looked in the direction of my creased and pressed Ashworth golf pants. "Uh, just wear jeans, and I'll get you a dozen of our company polo shirts. They have our logo on them. You can wear that every day so you won't have to worry about selecting outfits each morning."

"Okay, that'll be easy."

As I headed for the door, Richard added, "Oh, and get yourself a pair of steel-toed boots. It's better to wear those around here."

I walked into the office next door and looked for the new computer to determine which desk was mine. It was a small square office painted white, with desks at opposite ends of the room facing the side walls. The modest rectangular window on the far wall provided some natural relief from the bright fluorescents above. The desk to the right was clear of any papers, and sitting atop it were two new flat screen monitors. In front of the desk was a typical office chair free of rips or stains; it looked newly assembled. Settling down in the new chair, I noticed a fine layer of black dust on the desktop. I scanned over the work area and saw the thin layer of dust covering most everything in the office. The dust must have originated from the scrap metal being loaded on ships non-stop a thousand feet from the office. I didn't know what I was breathing but accepted the particulates. I was just happy to be employed, a productive human in the grind of life.

After the computer booted up, I scoured the Internet and found some free safety manual shareware. I deemed it safe to download the file after checking the reliability of the preloaded virus software.

While the loading bar shot the percentage of downloaded information, I thought about the blind jump I had made by taking the new job and wondered if it would help launch my life into a more enjoyable journey. Experience told me that geography wouldn't make my affliction go away. It would be inside until I booted it out. There was no magic to rid me of panic disorder, depression, or agoraphobia. Doctors so far had failed with medication and feel-good therapy. As the downloading of the safety manual shareware continued, I stared at the screen thinking about how nice it would be if the medical profession had a mental therapy that cured in the same way physical therapists helped heal accident victims.

Today we are going to do cranial water aerobics. The object here is to submerge your head underwater and spin around as fast as you can, while moving your neck up and down, banging it like you're at a death metal concert. This will work your panic muscle. Hold your breath as long as you can. The closer you get to drowning, the more therapeutic the workout. But before you dunk your head, put these shackles around your wrists. The shackles are attached to a half-ton brick to keep you under water. To unlock them, you must use the key attached to the right wrist cuff. Make sure to get the key loose and unlock yourself before you lose consciousness. Use your time wisely. But don't worry, our alert staff will pull you to safety if there are any problems. Now let's start our first session. The advanced seriousness of your condition warranted the doctor to prescribe this treatment once a day, every day, for six months. By then you should see tremendous improvement and maybe even be cured. It's all up to your dedication.

After a minute of daydreaming, I looked away from the download meter on my screen to see a large face with a beaming smile in the doorway.

"Mundo. What are you doing?" I asked.

"Hey, Wade. I heard you were over here. Looks like you're working hard, just staring at the computer. Does Richard know that?"

"That's my job, just sit here and stare. What are you doing?"

"I just wanted to stop and say goodbye. I'm moving to North Carolina tomorrow. Government duty calls, you know."

"Tomorrow? I didn't know it was that soon."

"Yeah, that soon. Come here and give me a hug before I go." Mundo opened his bulky forearms to receive me.

I stood up and led myself into his arms like a submissive child. "Short hug jughead, not a long one," I said.

With that, he squeezed me tight and lifted my body about three inches off the ground. "Yeah, I'll miss your cute face," Mundo said as he undid his tight embrace.

I stepped back a couple of feet from him and bowed my head. "Look, Mundo, thanks for taking me to Las Vegas and I'm sorry—"

"Say no more," Mundo interrupted. "I liked jumping on that guy. Probably the most exciting flight I've ever had."

"I'm glad you enjoyed it. I'll email you sometime."

"I'll believe it when I see it. I've got to go. I saw Richard earlier, but I just wanted to get in one last hug before I left."

"Thanks for thinking about me," I said.

15. The Encounter

The slip of paper with the Nardil prescription written on it sat on my kitchen counter for a week before I finally got it filled.

"Wade Hampton," I said to the pretty Hispanic pharmacist at Osco Drugs. She had filled my first installment of Xanax the day I drove back to Phoenix. I watched as she bent over to fetch the bottle, and it made me very aware that I didn't have any girlfriends to call up and curl next to. As she returned to the counter, I looked at her left hand to see no ring on the appropriate finger.

"Would you like to go out to dinner tonight?" I asked casually.

She glanced at the prescription for Nardil and smiled, but her look was more out of sympathy than friendliness. She probably knew Nardil was prescribed for people with real mental problems.

"I don't think so," she said.

I failed to produce my fake charming smile as I grabbed the bag and walked away with a couple more layers of esteem shaved off my skin. On the way out of the store, I ripped up the three-page disclaimer sheet included with the tinted plastic pill bottle, discarding the bits into a nearby trashcan.

I returned to my apartment at Capital Bluff and was conspicuously aware of the disorientation of my new surroundings. I went into the small bathroom to open the pill bottle and reveal its contents. This inspection process had become a habit years back when I started taking medications for panic and depression. I would study the pills, putting them close to my eyes like an entomologist examining an insect specimen.

The fifteen-milligram Nardil pills were bright orange and had a marking on one side stamped in black writing, "PD 270." I assumed the "PD" stood for Parke-Davis, the manufacturer of the drug, but had no idea what the numbers meant. The pills resembled the shape of an Advil pain reliever pill, but about twenty-five percent smaller.

The drug basically worked by inhibiting the process of neurotransmitters such as serotonin, dopamine and norepinephrine being killed by a protein in the brain called monoamine oxidase, or MAO. If the MAO "cleaning" function was too active in the brain, it could cause a lower level of these neurotransmitters and create a chemical imbalance known to cause depression.

I contemplated throwing a pill in my mouth but stopped my arm in mid-flight. If the drug made me tired, maybe I would let Richard down by not being able to perform my work duties. My anxiety was manageable as long as nothing out of the ordinary arose, but I noticed with the start of my new job and surroundings, it was beginning to rise again. After a flicker of debate, I convinced myself to hold off adding another drug on top of the Xanax. The orange blockers would have to wait.

* * * *

I was settling into a routine after a couple of weeks under my belt as director of administration for Haverco. As I was proofreading the final draft of the newly written safety manual, my mind wandered to the women in my past. My desperation for companionship was not consuming me as it had in Arizona, but once I became more settled in my new surroundings, my need would probably return. One night in weakness I attempted to phone Pamela, but her line was disconnected. Maybe she was telling the truth about moving to Michigan.

The harbor area wasn't exactly the prime spot for finding females. Potbellied longshoremen dominated the human landscape. There were no ladies to casually stand by the copy machine and chat with. The harbor was generally a man's domain – there were few female laborers, welders, or longshoremen. The only female employee at Haverco was Richard's part-time secretary, a married woman with three kids.

I took a break from reading the safety manual, bored with the long drawn-out chapter explaining exactly how to secure equipment on trucks. I strolled outside to the parking area and wafted through the black dust floating in the air from scrap metal being loaded on a nearby ship. A couple of cars down from mine, three women were leaning on an old white Pontiac Firebird. The first woman, Rosa Lopez, I'd met on my second day of employment. She was an already aging twenty-six-year-old longshoring groupie who, for nearly a decade, had broken up many a dockworker's marriage.

My eyes ran over to the second, a full-bodied girl I had seen once before, but never met. The third, farthest away from me, caught my eye as I did another quick survey of the trio. I performed a split-second double take because the other two girls didn't evoke any feral emotions. The third woman, upon a speedy second analysis, fomented an acute case of instant chemical attraction.

She had long black hair, straight with a touch of thick wave running down to her thin waist, and a slender, yet femininely muscular five-foot eight-inch frame. Her flawless olive skin and dark features gave her the mystique of an ethnic goddess.

As I moved closer, it was obvious she did not have the same primordial reaction to me. Her look was somewhat tough, though definitely not snobbish. It was clear she was not from the right side of the tracks, but that didn't bother me. I settled a few steps from the white Firebird adorned by one beauty and the two other women. Without waiting for a formal introduction, which was hard to come by from ladies who hung around the docks to meet longshoremen, I guided the question to Rosa and belted out cockily, "Who's this?"

"Her name's Sophia," Rosa said, as my eyes scanned the raven-haired splendor.

"Sophia?"

"Yes idiot, can't you hear?" the larger girl said. "Sophia. My older sister."

"She doesn't look like you."

"We had different fathers. But she still looks kinda' like me," she bellowed back.

"No she doesn't."

"She does too, Waaaade!"

"And you are?" I asked, trying to suppress the surprise that she knew my name.

"Alexa Syros," she snarled.

I decided not to encourage the "does not, does too" routine with Alexa, so I turned to Sophia and asked politely, "Is she your sister?"

"Sometimes," she said without enthusiasm.

"You want to go out with us tonight, Waaaade?" Alexa asked.

"Sounds like a plan. Where are you going?"

"We're going to Fathom's at about eight o'clock."

"I don't know if I'll go," Sophia said.

"Yes you will, bitch," Alexa responded, then hit her sister on the shoulder. "We'll meet you there, Wade."

"With Sophia?" I asked, directing my question to Alexa.

"Yeah, she'll go. She's just being a scrod."

The comment propelled Sophia to walk away from us and out to the bare pavement on the berth.

"Isn't a scrod a or something?" I asked.

"Uhh, yeah," Alexa said as if I should have known.

I turned away from Alexa and caught up with Sophia as she continued a slow walk toward the docked ship.

"Hi," I said.

"Hi," Sophia responded in a deep reserved tone.

Her acknowledging my presence gave me optimism, at least for the moment. As I stared at her intensely for an unacceptable amount of time, her eyeballs began shifting from side to side.

"What's the matter with you?" she asked with a slight laugh.

"Nothing, I just think you're beautiful."

Sophia cast a stern look, obviously not much for flattery. She studied me a moment, taking a long look at my ironed shirt and jeans before saying, "Fathom's is not the type of place you look like you'd go to typically."

"I'll go to see you," I said. "I don't care where we are."

"I'll go, just not for you. But at least now I know your intentions."

I laughed. "I didn't know people used the word 'intentions' anymore. Reminds me of some antebellum ritual of having to impress the matriarch before getting to hold hands with the daughter. But if you think I don't fit in, why don't we go to a place where the *fit* is better?"

"Let's not."

"Why not?"

"Not tonight."

Apparently, my sparse charm didn't take to Sophia. She turned away from me and headed to her Firebird.

I walked back to Alexa and Rosa and leaned to Alexa's ear. "Okay, I'll see you tonight. Make sure Sophia is there," I said.

"The bitch will be there," Alexa confirmed. "She likes you," she added.

"Likes me? I don't know about that."

Alexa gave her best coy smile, which came off as someone about to blow a lip fart. "She talked to you, she hasn't talked to any man for a long time."

Sophia was looking out to the waterfront, apparently uninterested in the exchange. Nonetheless, it was a date, new friends and all.

16. The Kiss

As I combed my hair in the bathroom preparing for my perceived date with Sophia and her friends, I noticed a lighter feeling in my mind. Anxiety still greeted me every morning, manifested in a ball of turmoil knotting my stomach. But I would manage to arrive at work, get busy, and forget about it for a while. It was always present, just not quite at the debilitating stage.

I went into my neatly arranged walk-in closet to find something to wear, moving slowly to buy some time to allow the mandatory ritual of letting some anticipatory anxiety set in, a standard operating procedure. The simple task of going out with new people in different surroundings conjured up all sorts of morbid scenarios. I became a creature of safety—always driving myself to an event or place, even if it meant I went alone. Having my own car gave me control and allowed a quick exit if I started panicking.

During my heightened periods of suffering from panic attacks, I would miss events because I wouldn't attend without my safety net—the getaway car. I also did not want to take others in case I had problems coping with the situation and begged to go home, only to spoil the fun they were having. And any form of public transportation was out of the question. This evolved into a withdrawal from situations and literally giving up friendships. It became such a burden to be with people, I shut many out. That led to loneliness, which was no more fun than anticipating having a substantial panic attack with friends.

Wherever I lived, I perceived home as kind of a *no panic zone*. My new apartment at Capital Bluff had quickly become that zone, as my house in Scottsdale had been before. I was by no means immune to anxiety and panic when at home; I just felt it was a safe zone and the best place to go if I needed to retreat.

Home was an escape route in my mind, not to be free of myself, but free from making a fool out of myself in front of other people. That was my ultimate fear, going crazy and pleading for help in front of strangers who, I felt, wouldn't care if I collapsed into insanity. Similar to the experience I had on the flight with Richard and Mundo. I preferred to be alone rather than involve witnesses. So I started enclosing myself.

Tonight though, I wanted to interact with Sophia. I recollected past companions and my mind wandered back to Pamela. Though it was quickly becoming lonely in Los Angeles, I affirmed that not getting married was the best decision I had ever made. I felt no guilt in the matter and questioned in hindsight why I hadn't mustered the courage to confront my lack of feelings for Pamela earlier in our relationship.

No guilt, no avoidance. My clothing was all nice and ironed. I walked to my car with confidence. It was time to head out and learn more about Sophia Syros.

When I arrived at Fathom's, one of many similar bars on Sixth Street in San Pedro, the place was glutted with the mainstay of the local retail community: longshoremen with their paychecks and a spattering of hipsters with money derived from unknown sources. The bar had an ample crowd for the eight o'clock hour.

Rosa and Alexa walked in five minutes after I arrived. Sophia trailed behind them by a couple of seconds. When she made her entrance, her jeans hugged her perfectly. A sheer black t-shirt enveloped her breasts and stretched across her firm stomach before disappearing into her pants.

"Waaaade!" Alexa belted out in her melodic baritone.

I kissed Alexa on the lips but decided not to venture putting a smack on Sophia while I had the momentum. Sophia's long dark hair was pulled back in a ponytail secured by a faded red bandana. I had only seen her with her hair straight down, but pulled away from her face revealed a beautiful jaw line, and soft ears perfectly sized for her head. Next to her, Rosa and Alexa were already gabbing with people at the bar.

"How about a drink?" I hailed an older female bartender. "Miss, get these lovely ladies whatever they want."

After Sophia got her Jack Daniels on the rocks, she eased away from the bar and worked her way through the expanding crowd. Sloughing off the ogles as she passed by a few men, she sat at an empty table. I swooped in to fill the seat across from her and set my Crown and water on the table.

"You have the most beautiful hair. And I love it pulled back with that bandana."

She twisted her head and touched the red cloth. "It's my lucky bandana."

"Sitting with you, I think I'm the lucky one tonight."

She looked away and sighed. Her face tensed as she ignored the comment.

"What's the matter, you have a boyfriend or something?" I asked.

"No," she replied immediately.

"Well, it'd be nice if you'd talk to me."

"I'll talk to you," she said. "Just give me something to talk about." The corners of her lips curled upward ever so slightly. To me, it was a welcome indication of some friendliness.

"Okay… where do you work?"

Sophia cocked her head. It looked like she was thinking, *is that the best you can do?* "I'm a teacher's assistant at Crestwood Elementary in San Pedro."

"Is that what you want to be—you know, a teacher's assistant?"

"I want to be a first-grade teacher because I love kids. But I don't have the money to get my teaching credential."

Sophia polished off the rest of the Jack in one large swig and sucked a small jagged ice cube into her mouth. She swirled her empty glass around and delivered a reserved wet-lipped smile. "If that answer suffices, how about getting me another one?"

I jumped out of my seat in a display of motivation I hadn't felt in ages and pushed through the crowd, receiving a couple of elbows to the ribs as I rushed to the bar for another Jack Daniels. At that rate, I decided to get two drinks, doubles in fact. When I came back to the table with drinks in both hands, Sophia was still sitting alone, her black hair shining from the track lights lining the walls above.

"So you love kids. Do you have any?" I asked as I sat back down.

"No," she answered with an exhale of mild shock. "Why would I have kids? I'm not married."

"Well, being married hasn't stopped a lot of people. And I didn't know if you'd been married before."

"No, I've never been married."

Alexa catapulted next to our table, interrupting the blossoming dialogue.

"You being good to my sister?" Alexa asked.

"As good as I can. Trying to get her to talk, you know?"

Alexa slapped Sophia on the shoulder. "Loosen up, bitch."

"I'm talking," Sophia said, then punched Alexa in the stomach. "Get out of here."

Alexa recoiled back a step and held her right side. "Beeyach," she said before leaving the table and latching on to a random guy.

"Let's see, what were we talking about?" I said, trying to keep the conversation going.

Sophia looked bored as she slumped back in her seat and crossed her arms. She stared at me momentarily with a blank gaze, perhaps calculating if the interaction was even worth her time. I looked away from Sophia and glanced at the bar crowd, averting my eyes for a couple of seconds before turning my head back to her.

"What?" I asked.

"Give me your hand." She sat back up and placed her elbows on the table. "I hate question and answer sessions. I'll learn more about you by reading your hand."

I jutted my right hand in front of her with the palm up. "Okay, read it. What am I all about?"

She fixed her eyes on my palm for a moment, then gently grabbed my hand and twisted it so the palm was facing downward. "I read the back of hands, not the palms."

I couldn't help laughing. "The back of hands? There aren't any of those lines on the back."

"There are plenty of lines on the back of your hand, they're just more subtle. You also don't have very discernible veins on the palm. The veins are very important. Are you right-handed?"

"Yes."

"Place it flat on the table with your fingers spread."

"Are we going to do something weird? I hope so," I said.

Her eyes met mine. With a look of emotional detachment, she said, "The hands never lie."

I slapped my hand on the table. She studied it for a moment and adjusted my fingers so they were fanned apart equidistant to each other. Her long fingers tickled my skin, and I felt a tingle run straight down to my crotch. Sophia leaned over the table, putting her face about a foot away from my splayed hand. She traced the tops of the larger veins delicately with her index finger, and then ran her fingertip down the sides of each digit. The soft touch was sensual, like some variety of ancient mystic foreplay. It began to drive me crazy—in a good way.

"First of all," Sophia began, "you have a round scar between your middle and ring finger."

"That's what happens when your fist collides with a brick wall."

"That is your love crevice," she said.

"No, I don't think so. I've been with enough women to know all the crevices I love."

Sophia managed a regulated grin, but did not take her eyes off my hand.

"There has been difficulty in past loves," she noted, "though your digital venous arch is protruding on your ring finger. So basically you are very sensual, but feel no love."

"My Venus arch is protruding?" I looked down at my pants. "It is not."

She kept scrutinizing my hand, ignoring the joke. "Your cephalic vein is more subdued. That's a sign of intelligence."

"Did you say phallic? I think you're turning me on."

"Maybe I was wrong about the intelligence part." She ran her finger across my skin. "Your knuckles show some stress, like you've worked with your hands at some point. Not in an artistic way, but more from labor."

"Well, I did own an auto detailing shop before I moved here." I held up my left hand and moved it in a rapid circular motion. "You know—wax on, wax off?"

"I get it," she said. "The lines between your thumb and index finger chronicle your life into a pattern of early prosperity, then sadness, then chaos—but will stabilize ultimately."

Her analysis made my joking halt abruptly. I was now concerned about the 'sadness' and 'chaos' part. "When will it stabilize?"

Sophia nodded her head. "I don't know, but someday."

"I hope I'm not dead by then."

Slowly, she shifted her eyes to me. "Oh, you won't be."

"Okay, tell me more," I said.

Her fingers worked the top of my hand as if she were reading Braille. A strange look materialized on her face. She cocked her head slightly and went into deep thought.

"You see the protruding vein running up to that scar? That's a dorsal metacarpal vein. It's a little lump that disappears suddenly. This means you have untapped vitality, but something is holding you back."

My shoulders became tight. I was trying to come up with a snappy response, but I just looked at her. She glanced at me quickly before returning her gaze to my right hand.

"That line right there," she pointed by the knuckle below my index finger, "shows there has been some sadness surrounding you. Not just things in life that happen, but something of pleasure has been taken away."

"Yeah," I murmured, thinking about traveling. "Man, this is now getting me depressed."

Sophia smiled. "Here, let me find a happier line." She twirled her middle finger above my hand, teasing me with her next analysis. "You see that last line on your pinky?"

I leaned over the table, our heads just an inch apart. "Yeah, I see it."

"Well that line says, 'Please get Sophia another drink.'" She kissed my forehead. A full smile appeared on my face while she sat back in her seat a bit and crossed her arms. I got her two more drinks and hurried back to the table.

"Here's your drink—or drinks."

"Thank you," Sophia said.

"So… are you done displaying your impressive hand reading talents?"

"For now, yes."

I took a small sip of my Crown Royal and water, which was mostly water due to my slow drinking pace. Sophia downed the first of her two fresh drinks.

"So besides reading the back of hands, what else do you like to do?" I asked.

Sophia placed her glass on the table next to the full one. "I love to read. I read about two books a week. It's my great escape."

"Who's your favorite author?"

"I really don't have a favorite, but if I were to pick one, I'd say Anais Nin."

"That's pretty erotic stuff. You're turning me on again."

She didn't react except for a slight downward tip of her head.

"Hey, let me read your hand," I said.

"I'd like that, but you don't know how to," Sophia replied. I fired off my best groveling look. She watched the act for a few seconds before putting her right hand on the table. "Okay, go ahead."

I stared at her beautiful hand. Her long fingers and flawless skin sat flat on the table. I stroked my fingers across the top as I looked into her eyes to see some kind of reaction. She sat patiently, letting me take in the feel of her skin.

"This isn't fair. You don't have any veins sticking out like I do."

"That's because skin thins as you age, and the veins become more prominent."

"How old are you?"

"Twenty-eight."

"You're a year older than me," I said.

"But I've lived a clean life."

"That explains it," I said. "Your hands are beautiful. You could be a hand model. I mean, even your fingernails are perfect."

"You going to read, or are you just going to admire?"

"I want to do both at the same time." I moved my face closer to her hand. "I would say from the only vein I can see, that you are very sensual, yet repressed. Like you need something… something someone can provide."

"Like you?" Sophia said facetiously.

"Yeah, exactly." I put my nose to her fingers. "And your hand smells good, real good. That's the sign of a clean soul."

"Smell is not a part of hand reading."

"What about taste?" I kissed the top of her fingers one by one, starting with her pinky and working my way to her thumb. Sophia didn't move her hand. "They taste good too."

She pulled her hand away carefully. "You're woefully lacking in hand reading, but pretty good at finger arousal."

"Maybe I just found my next career."

As I felt a spark had ignited between us, a younger male made a quick entrance into the bar and sat warily on a solitary chair a few feet away from our table. A decent looking guy, his eyes shifted over us and passed across casually. Sophia glanced his way and quickly leaned over the table close to me.

"That's my old boyfriend," Sophia said in a loud whisper. "Act like you're my boyfriend now, I don't want to talk to him. He still wants me."

She rushed around the small table, wrapped her right arm tightly around me, and knelt down far enough so our faces were level. Then to my surprise, her smooth wet tongue deeply struck my mouth, pushing my head back in astonished delight.

I proceeded to take advantage of this by dancing my tongue around hers, creating a mesmerizing kiss that must have lasted half a minute. I opened my eyes long enough to see the old boyfriend zeroed-in on us. After a few seconds of watching he exited the bar, pushing open the front door with angry force and disappearing into the street.

Alexa, along with other people in our proximity who spectated the two of us intertwined, cheered us on as we made out. Rosa missed the spectacle. She too was getting some action at the end of the black fake-marble bar spanning the side wall. Her arms were dangling around some guy, lips in motion. Alexa had also hooked up with a married guy who served as an occasional sexual satisfier when the feeling struck. They were working each other with rekindled interest.

When we gained our composure after the extended kiss, Alexa approached the two of us as we resumed our original positions across the table from one another.

"Wade, I've got my man for the night and Rosa is going to stick around here. Why don't the four of us go back to your apartment? You might get laid," Alexa shouted into my ear.

I turned my head to ask Sophia, "If you go with us to my apartment, will I get laid?"

Out of embarrassment, she gave Alexa a look of sisterly hatred. She shifted her eyes to me and dropped a bombshell that I least expected. With an expressionless face, she coolly replied, "Maybe."

"You better use it Soph, or else it'll dry up," Alexa said.

"Let's go!" I said before Sophia and Alexa could get into a brawl and put an end to our impending interlude.

Alexa gathered up her married man, a guy named Tony, and the four of us went back to my apartment.

17. The Love

"Thanks for letting me and my guy friend use your living room last week," Alexa said. "I'm glad Sophia finally got laid," she added.

I hadn't seen Alexa since our night at Fathom's. She was hanging around the docks socializing with longshoremen on their breaks. Most of the harbor waterside area was inaccessible to the public, but the facility at the Blue Berth was one of the last remaining unguarded entrances, and Alexa took advantage of that. Her free reign of the docks had limited time due to the planned security upgrade at the berth.

"What do you mean 'finally got laid?'" I asked.

"It's been like eight years for her. I was getting worried."

"Eight years? No way."

"I'm not shittin' you, Wade. She's only been with one guy in her life, and that was when I was still in high school."

"I don't believe that."

"No, it's true. She went out with him for a couple of years, then caught him fucking some other chick. I'm glad you got together with her. She's been a lot less bitchy since she spent the night with you."

"Did she say anything?"

"No, but that's not surprising. I know she likes you though, or else she wouldn't have spread her legs, no matter how drunk she was."

"She really likes me?"

"Of course she does, stupid. You should call her up and take her out tonight."

Alexa gave me her phone number and I ran into my office to give Sophia a call.

Instead of Sophia's silky voice on the phone, a standardized electronic female voice greeted me. *"We're sorry, the number you have dialed has been disconnected, or is no longer in service..."*

Confused, I looked at the receiver as if it had made a mistake. I redialed, only to hear the same woman robot delivering the identical message. I walked back outside to find Alexa.

"I called the number, but it's disconnected."

Alexa puffed up her large chest as she shoved her hand in her jeans pocket, retrieved her phone and confirmed the service outage. Little creases formed around her pursed lips as she prepared for the outburst. "That old bitch!"

"Who, Sophia?"

"No, my mom. She didn't pay the phone bill again."

"Why would your mom have to pay Sophia's phone bill?"

"We all live together and are on the same phone plan. She was supposed to cover the bill last month, but the dumbshit didn't pay it again. Our cell phones work on and off because of her."

"How about if I go and visit her in person instead?"

"Yeah, go do that," Alexa said. "I'll give you the address."

* * * *

After work, I drove to the south side of San Pedro, making a stop at a neighborhood liquor store owned by a Korean family. White plastic buckets filled with small bouquets of flowers lined the front door—varieties of carnations, daisies, and a few dwarfed roses. I picked out two bunches of flowers, hoping Sophia would like at least one of the bouquets.

Their apartment was near 34th Street and Peck. A peek of the Pacific in the form of a blue three-quarter square was visible through the rows of small houses and apartments sloping gently down the coastal hill. As I drove by the white two-story building, I saw Sophia's Firebird parked on the street and parallel parked behind her car. With the flowers in my hand, I walked the building from one end to the other until I located unit number eight, the downstairs corner apartment.

I rapped on the door three times. A moment later I was greeted by a woman about fiftyish with black hair and dark eyes that blended into her olive skin like a doll figurine. She had the presence of having been very attractive in her younger years, but daily life and extended birthdays had tugged at her face. Her expression was classic premature aging—the culmination of hard work and unfulfilled expectations.

"Hello. I'm Wade Hampton, and I'm here to visit Sophia." I lifted the flowers in my left hand.

"Oh, my," she said. A nervous smile crept upon her face.

A piercing voice came from inside the apartment. "That's Wade, Sophia's new man. Don't just keep him standing out there. Let him in, Mom."

"I'm letting him in, Alexa. Please don't shout." She took a step back to let me pass through the narrow doorway. "I'm Barbara Syros, Sophia's mother," she said, staring down at the two modest bouquets.

"Nice to meet you, Ms. Syros."

I walked around a small partition by the front door. The bare off-white walls of the apartment's interior contrasted the well-used furniture encapsulated in time from the 1980s. Alexa was sitting on a tattered turquoise cloth couch with marred black lacquered wood armrests, watching a rerun of some millennial reality show on the small television.

"Hey Wade," Alexa said. "Sorry you had to come over here, but my mom forgot to pay the phone bill again."

Barbara flushed with embarrassment. Her hand draped across her chest, appalled by Alexa's accusation. "I didn't forget, there was just a mix-up at the bank," she said.

"No, you just forgot to pay the bill. Alzheimer's must be setting in."

"Alexa! I'm telling you, there was a mistake at the bank."

"Sure there was, Mom." Alexa turned her head and looked at me. "She pulls this crap all the time."

"Alexa!"

In one quick motion, Barbara drew her body inward like a dog about to receive a swatting. She looked at me with desperation as I stood rigid, not wanting to get in the middle of a mother-daughter catfight.

"Is Sophia here?" I asked Barbara, trying to diffuse an impending argument.

"Yes, she's in her bedroom, probably reading. She's always reading. I'm sure she heard you come in, but she's a little shy."

"I wouldn't call her shy," I said. "Maybe a bit mysterious."

Barbara smiled. "It's in her genes. Her father was a brilliant man. He was an engineer. Many of Sophia's mannerisms come from him."

"Where's her father?"

"He died before Sophia was one-year-old." She sighed. "A motorcycle accident."

"Oh… I'm sorry." I lowered my voice. "So that's why Sophia and Alexa have different fathers. I guess that explains the sibling difference."

"Yes." She turned her head to Alexa. "Alexa's father is a stupid bum," she whispered. "That's why Alexa took the Syros name. I should have never married him. But, I was a young widow with a child at the time, and he came along during a vulnerable period."

I glanced at Alexa's large frame settled on the couch, not knowing if she could hear the conversation. She was staring at the TV, momentarily oblivious to our presence.

Barbara darted her eyes to a closed door at the end of the hallway. "But Sophia... she's the most loving and caring person I've ever seen. She does have a way of putting up a cold wall around her, especially around new people." Barbara moved her head closer as if she were going to tell me a secret. "You know, she's been hurt before by a man."

I shifted my eyes over to the couch where Alexa sat. "I know."

Barbara walked to the end of the hallway and knocked on the door. There was a nervousness to her, some kind of built-up franticness from living with her two grown daughters—an arrangement she probably would have never envisioned years ago when their baby teeth were still intact.

"Sophia, Wade Hampton is here to see you."

Without hesitation or engaging in a dramatic waiting pause, Sophia opened the door and peered down the hallway. She approached me with no expression as I scanned her beautiful body covered with a black t-shirt and skin-hugging white bicycle shorts. Her black hair flowed across her breasts as if purposefully set there. Though she was clad in the most unassuming garb, the only thing I could think was how stunning she looked.

"Hi. I... brought you these." I lifted the flowers.

"Thank you."

It appeared she appreciated the gift, but her external reaction was hard to gauge. She walked into the small galley kitchen and grabbed a large-mouthed plastic cup out of the cabinet. With delicate care, she removed the rubber band holding the stems together and one at a time, placed each flower in the cup, arranging them to her liking before filling the makeshift vase with water.

As Barbara and I stood and watched Sophia tend to her flowers, Alexa sat up on the couch and grabbed a cigarette out of her purse.

"Alexa, I told you not to smoke in here," Barbara scolded.

Alexa leaned back on the couch and flicked her lighter. "I can smoke in here if I want to. I pay a third of the rent."

"No, you cannot smoke in here. You know Sophia and I don't like the smoke."

"Oh, be quiet," Alexa shouted. "I'll smoke in here if I want to."

Barbara threw up her hands. "God in heaven, I don't know how much more of this I can take."

While Sophia walked back to her bedroom with the flowers, Barbara stormed over to the kitchen and started cleaning a sink full of dishes. She whispered to herself, obviously about the less than ideal living arrangements. Alexa remained on the couch puffing away on a Marlboro.

Sophia emerged from her room a moment later. I noticed she had tied her hair into a ponytail with the red bandana she wore the night at Fathom's.

"Take me away from this," she said with unruffled control as she walked past me.

I looked at Alexa, then Barbara. Both fixed their attention on me, waiting for a response.

"Okay. You want to go eat?" I asked.

"I'm not really hungry. But I'll go with you to eat."

"I would enjoy that." I turned to Barbara. "Very nice to meet you."

"You kids have a good time," she said as I opened the front door.

I could feel the eyes of Barbara and Alexa watching us through the window as we walked to the car. I opened the door for Sophia, and with grace not common in women from her social standing, she settled into the car seat. I kept her door open and leaned over closer to Sophia.

"You know what kind of car this is?" I asked, giving her a little quiz to determine if she had any Pamela-like shallowness to her.

She looked around the inside of the car until she found the logo in the middle of the steering wheel. "It's a BMW. At least that's what the steering wheel says. I'm not much into cars."

"Good." I closed the door gently.

I got into the car and maneuvered out of the parallel parking space.

"How about Mexican food at Poquito Gato?" I asked.

"Sounds okay."

"All right… I'll have you there in a couple of minutes."

The moment we walked into Poquito Gato, I recalled the last time I was there. It was the night I boarded the fateful flight to Vegas with Richard and Mundo. As Sophia and I sat across from each other in a secluded booth, my mind worked feverishly to overcome the pre-panic signals shooting throughout my body. The bar encounters didn't bother me as much, but eating was different. Confined to a table and stuck for the whole meal was always a catalyst for distress. Two glasses of water were on the table and I immediately took a sip from one.

"So, you want a drink?" I asked.

"No, I'll just have water. I really don't drink much. Last week at Fathom's was an exception."

"Did you have a good time that night?"

Sophia's eyes squinted. "You mean: Did I have a good time when we went back to your apartment?"

"Uh… yeah. Yeah, when we were at my apartment. That's what I meant."

"Yes, I did. You made me feel good," she said, her poker face intact.

"Well, I heard you hadn't done that for like eight years."

"What?" Her poker face vanished. "Where did you hear that?"

"Alexa told me."

"God, Alexa has an overactive mouth."

"So, is it true?"

She took a calculated sip of her water, perhaps stalling before opening herself up.

"Yes, it's true. When I was twenty, I went out with a guy who I thought I was going to marry. I went over to his apartment one day and he was in bed with one of his female neighbors. We broke up after that."

"What about that guy at Fathom's the other night—you said he was an old boyfriend?"

Sophia refolded her napkin before placing it on her lap. "He wasn't really an old boyfriend." She smiled and guided her eyes down to the pale yellow tablecloth. "We only went out on one date, but he kept calling and texting. I wasn't interested in seeing him again. Nothing wrong with him, I just wasn't attracted."

"I'm glad you blew it out of proportion, it led to a very nice kiss—and a great night."

"You got lucky, that's all," she said.

"I did? You were the one wearing your *lucky* red bandana."

"True." She turned her head and touched the bandana.

The waitress came by to take our order. Sophia didn't order any food. I was surprised because most women I had dated, either to be fashionable or out of some updated rule of etiquette, always claimed they weren't hungry before going to a restaurant. Yet when they got there, suddenly they acquired a pang for some exotic appetizer or a super-sized salad. I ordered a gringo burrito. My stomach started to rumble as I handed the menu back to the waitress. The feeling was familiar. It was a panic attack waiting to mushroom throughout my body. Fear mode immediately initiated.

"Uh… so how do you like living with your mom and sister?" I managed to ask despite the increased thumping in my head. It was so irritating knowing what was going to happen. My panic was tenacious, tedious and frustratingly predictable.

"It's tolerable for now. My mom and Alexa argue almost constantly, but they're family and I can deal with it. It helps with the bills since none of us make much money."

I put my right palm to my forehead and rubbed it across the top of my head, making my hair stand up for a moment. As panic poked at my skin, I repeated the stroke across the top of my head.

"Uh… I'm sorry about your father. Your mom told me," I said, as air chopped its way down my throat. Hyperventilation was commencing.

"I was too young to remember him. I feel sorry for my mother, though. She never really recovered after—" She looked at me with puzzlement as I plunged half my napkin in a glass of water and wiped my face. "Are you all right?" she asked.

My deep breathing made it difficult to speak. "I don't feel very good."

"Are you sick?" she asked in a soothing, unthreatening way.

"You... could say that. But not in the traditional sense."

Sophia rose from her side of the booth and sat next to me. I could feel the warmth of her hips touching mine. "Do you have some kind of condition—seizures, heart trouble or something?" She gripped my hand. Her soft skin caressed the tops of my fingers.

"No." I gulped in a short breath. "It's different, not physical. I don't know how to explain it."

She softened her grip on my hand as I closed my eyes and tried to get my heart rate down. I opened my eyes a crack and saw Sophia studying me with concern.

"Look at me," Sophia instructed.

I turned to her and looked in the way a frightened little boy would when seeking comfort from his mother. She squeezed my hand.

"I'm with you, everything will be fine," she said.

"Are you sure?" I moaned.

"Yes. We're just eating in a restaurant, having a good time. If you really get sick, I can go get help. But for now, I'll be here next to you."

Those simple words flourished two or three times in my mind. Her calmness brought me to a state of reality, to the juncture of the legitimate safety of the here and now. No one had ever quieted my mind with such understated passion—and such speed. It was as though Sophia understood what I was experiencing, despite the fact she had absolutely no knowledge of my condition. As we sat next to each other waiting for my burrito, it felt like most of the negative weight vaporized out the top of my head, leaving room for repressed enjoyment to fill the space. I glanced apprehensively at Sophia and could see nothing but composed confidence in her eyes. She was the first person to ever get through to me, and she did it so effortlessly---almost as if Sophia had talents in some unpracticed, yet graceful psychology. My mind automatically tried to force the panic back in, but it halted abruptly. I didn't know what had just happened, but the only words that flashed in my mind were: *Dr. Crouch, I've found my mulch*.

18. The Apron

"So… how is it going with the Nardil?" Dr. Crouch asked.

"I haven't started taking it yet."

He twirled his mustache for a moment and followed it with a gentle circular rub on his temple.

"Why haven't you taken it yet?"

"Well, I'm having a problem with taking another drug. I mean, I'm already on Xanax."

"Have you been experiencing panic attacks in the past month?"

"Yes," I admitted. "I had one in a restaurant while on a date. I had one while driving over the Vincent Thomas Bridge in the harbor, I had one while lying on my bed, I even had one on the freeway when I was coming here. I wish your office was closer than Beverly Hills."

"You mean, you wish it was in your safety zone so you wouldn't have to face the challenge," Dr. Crouch stated.

I sat in silence, examining my knees. Dr. Crouch shifted his slender frame in his chair, leaning forward until his elbows rested on his knees.

"Look, Wade, I know you don't like coming here, or psychiatrists in general, but you need to change your behavior, break the cycle of panic and depressed states. If you're not willing to take the medication as prescribed, I don't know what else I can do. You don't want to attend endless therapy sessions, and frankly you're such a hardened case that medication is not only needed, but it's also almost mandatory if you're going to lead a normal life again."

"Well, I carry a stock of Xanax and Nardil with me at all times." I pulled out a small weatherproof wallet out of my left front pocket. "But I just haven't taken the Nardil yet."

Dr. Crouch inspected the wallet from across the office as I opened the Velcro-protected pouch to reveal the pills.

"You always carry that with you?"

"Yes, always."

"A safety net," Dr. Crouch noted.

"Sometimes I'm not at home when it's time to take the Xanax, so I found this much easier."

"Does it make you feel better to carry the pills with you at all times?"

I nodded my head sheepishly. "I guess so."

"If you carry it around with you, why don't you take the Nardil?"

"I would, but things are changing for me. You know that body mulching thing you told me about last time?"

"Have you tried it?"

"Well no, not exactly. But the exercise did come to me when I was out on a date. And now I feel much better. I think I'm in love."

Dr. Crouch's head jolted back. "In love? Weren't you supposed to get married just a couple of months ago?"

"Yeah, but I'm realizing that was a fluke. This woman is wonderful and I'm feeling better—at least when I'm around her."

"How long have you been going out with this woman?"

"Steadily, about a month now."

"That's a pretty short time frame, though I'm happy for you, Wade. But a woman, or love, won't solve your problems. This is a medical disease you have. And even if you do feel better with her, what are you going to do when she's not around?"

"I don't know. But I think things are changing," I said.

"Well by all means change. But go through the change with the help of the medication, along with your new *love*." Dr. Crouch lifted out of his seat. "Our time is up. But promise me you'll take the Nardil."

"I'll try."

Going back to my office after the appointment, I hit some construction on the 405 Freeway just south of Culver City. I didn't like getting stuck in traffic, there was nowhere to escape. Guiding my car to the right-hand lane in case I wanted to make a quick exit down the emergency lane, I realized that Dr. Crouch was probably correct in his assessment. I needed to go through the change. As my breathing got heavier, I put down my window to squeeze additional air into the car. I tried to envision some fresh shredded cedar mulch covering my body. The feeling made me itch, all that splintery wood stuck on me, suffocating my pores. I imagined my shirt and pants getting all crumpled from the ensuing wood chips. As my breathing increased, the wood chips felt as if they were covering my lips. I started spitting as I exhaled, trying to imagine the mulch breaking free from my lips and airway. I crammed my hand into my left front pocket to fetch a Nardil from the protective pill-holding wallet.

The sweat from my hand began to smudge the pill coating immediately. I closed my eyes tightly as the traffic in front of me went from a slow crawl to a dead stop. After thirty motionless seconds, I heard the courteous toot of a car horn from behind and I opened my eyes slowly. Cars in other lanes were moving ahead as the bottleneck of metal and plastic had come to an end. I wanted the panic to swirl out the window as I pushed on the gas pedal, but it wasn't abating. I looked down at the Nardil in my hand, accumulated some spit in my mouth, and swallowed the orange pill.

* * * *

When I arrived back at the office in the late afternoon after my appointment with Dr. Crouch, my phone rang just as I collapsed my legs to sit down.

"I'll have dinner waiting for you when you get home," Sophia said in a deep, measured voice. "And I'm going to serve it to you wearing only an apron."

"In that case, I'm glad I gave you a key to the place."

"When are you going to be here?"

"When do you want me?" I asked.

"I want you right now." The double entendre was not lost on her. "But the earlier you get home, the better it'll taste."

"What'll taste better?"

"The dinner *and* me."

"Ohhhhh." I glanced at my watch. "It's just after four. Will everything still taste good at the late hour of five?"

"I'll make sure it'll be even better by then."

As I hung up the receiver, Richard popped his head through the doorway.

"Hey Wade, did you open pension accounts for those new employees?"

"Yeah, I did that yesterday. They're all set up with the benefits package."

"Good." Richard entered the room and sat down on the chair across from me. "What else is going on?"

"Sophia just called. She cooked dinner and is going to serve it to me wearing only an apron."

Richard laughed while giving his knee a hard slap. "I don't know how you do that. Can I come over?"

"Sure, join us."

"No, that's all right. I'd have to ask my wife for permission first."

We both chuckled for a moment, Richard a little longer than I did, tipping me off he had something on his mind. He swung his chair to face me directly.

"Wade, I'm glad you're enjoying yourself and have a woman. I don't know Sophia personally, but she's Alexa's sister and all—"

"I know what you're thinking, but she's not the least bit like Alexa."

"Yeah, she's a hell of a lot better looking," Richard said.

"That, for one thing. But she's also very smart—she's totally different from Alexa. They had different fathers, so actually they're half-sisters. I know she doesn't have the social graces of the girls we grew up with, but that's because she was never exposed to that world—maybe for the better."

"Maybe."

Richard leaned back in the chair and folded his hands atop his head. I mimicked the same pose.

"You know," Richard said, "I always dreamed of being with a girl who came from nothing, and how I'd be able to give her more than she ever imagined. Kind of like a fairytale story. And here I ended up with a wife from a super-wealthy family. She was used to a certain standard of living. It worried me at first if I would be able to provide the kind of life for her that she grew up with. But looking back, it's turned out better than I could have ever imagined."

I thought back to his wisdom on the drive from Las Vegas. "Is this another one of those 'doily' speeches?"

"In a way, yes. Make sure you don't shit on your doily by getting overly involved with women from the wrong side of town."

"Does it matter which side of town she comes from? Sounds a little prejudicial."

"Don't throw the class card at me, Wade. Look, I didn't have you move to California to get mixed up with another problem. Women seem to cause you more harm than good."

"So… I didn't realize when you gave me a job, you'd also be monitoring my dating habits."

Richard shook his head and rolled his eyes. "If Sophia is a great gal, then it's all right. But you deserve someone who's going to make you feel better than you ever have—and I'm not talking in pussy-language—it's deeper than that."

Richard and I locked eyes and stared at each other for an uncomfortable amount of time. We'd been close friends for so long we could do this without feeling weird from the silence or lack of eye movement. Finally Richard gave in, blinked his eyes, and belted out a laugh.

"Okay, go home and get served by a naked woman. Promise to text me pictures if she lets you take any."

Within thirty minutes I was speeding up the hill on Capital Avenue, snaking around cars to shorten the drive home. I walked through the front door and noticed the coffee table in front of the new leather couch was set with two black pillar candles, bamboo placemats, a full complement of utensils, wine glasses filled with ice water, and two square throw pillows positioned on the floor below. For lack of a dining table, Sophia transformed the coffee table into a romantic culinary arena. I could smell a combination of spices intermingling with a sweet sugary aroma.

"I'm home."

"Perfect timing," Sophia said. With her back turned to me, she peered into the oven. Three bowed straps left a six-inch gap in the back of her black apron. The naked skin tease was a beautiful sight as she remained in the bent over position staring intently into the oven. "When you're cleaned up, go ahead and sit down on the pillow at the head of the table."

After washing my hands in the bathroom, I returned to the living room and sat cross-legged on the pillow as Sophia had instructed and sat in silence. She remained in the kitchen performing the finishing touches on the dinner. A minute later, I heard the delicate patter of her bare feet on the carpet.

"This is asparagus with a corn and tomato salsa, drizzled with Rose Queen dressing," she said. She set one plate at the top right corner of the placemat in front of me, and the other at her setting.

Sophia turned around after depositing the plates to reveal her bare backside. My eyes zeroed in on her buttocks, perfectly shaped and unblemished twin orbs. I pushed my hands on the floor to lift my body and jutted my head forward, planting a kiss on her right cheek.

"Beautiful," I commented.

"The asparagus?" she turned and said.

"I was actually talking about your ass."

"Oh," she whispered deeply. "The back of me looks good?"

"Good enough to eat."

"Well, why don't you start with the asparagus."

She smiled and walked into the kitchen, giving me an extended head-to-toe back view. I waited on my pillow as she returned with two large plates.

"For the entrée, we have spinach enchiladas on wheat tortillas, adrift in crema de chile, and on the side are three small homemade sweet tamales, because you're so sweet."

I looked down at the full plate with the enchiladas, covered in jack cheese and a white cream-based sauce, then focused on the tamales. The tamales were not wrapped in the traditional restaurant way, rather the corn husks were wrapped more like cough lozenges, twisted at both ends.

"Wonderful," I said. "This looks great. Where does a Greek girl learn how to cook Mexican?"

"My grandmother on my mom's side was from Mexico. So we grew up with this kind of food."

Sophia settled on her pillow while I ate all of my asparaguses. The Rose Queen dressing hit my taste buds with a spark—a tangy sweet oil and vinegar sensation.

"Do you wish for anything else before I start eating?" Sophia asked as she unruffled her napkin and placed it on her lap.

"I wish you'd wear that apron every night."

"Not very practical for everyday use, but I'll keep it in mind."

I had already dug into the spinach enchiladas when I remembered that I had just started taking Nardil that afternoon. Cheese was a forbidden food item while on the drug, it was even in bold print on the disclaimer I had ripped up. I tried to shrug it off, savoring the meal too much to worry about drug side effects. But apprehension about the Nardil instilled an anxiety shot. I was also beginning to feel somewhat tired, not in a "hard day's work" way, but more in the way of a groggy drunken stupor. I kept eating without a pause until the food was gone.

"Will you please spend the night again?" I beseeched her as I chewed the last bite of sweet tamale.

"You know, that'll make seven nights in a row," Sophia noted.

"Really? It doesn't seem like it. Is that too much closeness?"

"No, not really. I was hoping I could stay over tonight anyway. I called my mom to make sure the phone bill was paid this month—and it was—but my mom and Alexa were having another argument when I called. When they're really going at each other, it gets hard to sleep."

"Yeah, I don't know how you put up with the shrieking."

"I don't know. They're just two angry women. My mom is a nervous wreck, and Alexa sometimes takes advantage of that."

"Well, I'm glad you want to spend the night. I hope you're not doing it solely to get away from your mother and sister."

"No, that's not why. The main reason is to be with you, the family's another situation." Sophia cocked her head temperately and asked, "You like me being here?"

"Yes. In fact, I think we should shoot for seventy nights in a row, by that time we'll know if we are meant to be together."

"Seventy nights starting when?"

"I'll prorate you the past six nights, so we've got sixty-four nights left."

"That'll take us into August," Sophia noted. "What about after that?"

My mind slowed down during dinner, perhaps from the satiating food or the combination of Nardil and Xanax. "I don't know... but it will be fun finding out," I said, noticing a faint involuntary slur in my voice.

"Are you tired or something?"

"Yeah, I think so." I closed my eyes for a couple of seconds and then reopened them. "I started taking some medication today and I think it's making me tired."

Sophia pursed her lips before responding. "I saw the pill bottles in the bathroom. I know what Xanax is. I have some friends who like to take that. The other one—Nardil?—I don't know what that's for."

In the past, I would have deemed this as snooping in my personal things, but with Sophia, it didn't seem to disturb me. The lack of agitation surprised my cerebral senses for a moment; the thought that I was getting emotionally close to someone, like actually being a true, trusting couple. It was foreign to me.

"You remember the night at Poquito Gato and a few other times when you said I looked like something was wrong?"

Sophia nodded.

"That's what they're for," I said. "Also, I'm not supposed to have any cheese because of a drug interaction."

"Well, you just ate a lot of cheese," Sophia said as her eyes directed downward to my empty plate. "You'll need to tell me these things."

"That's okay, it was awesomely delicious. I'll take the risk."

"Then from now on I'll make you the best non-cheese meals you've ever had."

Sophia lifted herself from the pillow seat and bent down behind me. She nestled her hands under my armpits and lifted me to my feet. Her strength surprised me as she guided me to the couch. I let my body settle in the leather as she gently lowered me.

"You rest while I clean up the kitchen. Then I'll take my apron off and wake you up."

"I can hardly wait," I said.

Sophia stepped back slowly to prolong the view of her body, then turned her head and said in a lowered, yet confident tone, "After seventy nights of me, you won't need drugs anymore."

19. The Pact

"Happy twentieth night together," I declared to Sophia as I finished the last bite of my no-cheese lasagna dinner.

"I didn't know you were counting, but that's right, it is our twentieth straight night."

I learned in a very short time that Sophia prided herself on having a home-cooked meal ready when I returned from work. She got off from her teacher's assistant job at noon three times a week. In addition to making dinner, on the long afternoons she would write very suggestive letters I looked forward to reading when I came home.

"I didn't know lasagna could be made without cheese."

Sophia grinned. "When you put love into your cooking, anything can be made."

"You put *love* in your cooking for me?" I asked.

"Of course. I'm following an online list of forbidden foods you can't eat while taking Nardil. That way, you won't get a massive headache like you did the night you ate those enchiladas." She disappeared around the small wall beside the kitchen entry. "I'll keep you healthy—except for the banana cream pie I made for dessert."

"I can eat bananas? I thought that was on the list?"

Sophia came out from behind the kitchen wall and shook her head evenly. "It is on the list, but it's just the little strings in the crevices of the bananas that are bad. You know those thin strands that kind of pull off when you peel them? I removed all of the strings from them before I made the pie."

"Wow," I said to myself.

"Are you tired?" she asked.

I blew out a breath and sat on the couch. "Yeah, a little bit. I think my body's still getting used to that Nardil."

She withdrew her head from sight again, but I continued staring in her direction. I thought about our concentrated, yet intimate relationship that showed no early indication of distress. The yearning to be with her all the time conflicted with the apprehensive second-guesses I had about jumping into cohabitation—especially since I was engaged to Pamela just a couple of months before. I held to my beliefs that Sophia was as genuine as she seemed and wouldn't become just another female lapse of judgment on my part. While I was still staring, she walked out of the kitchen and nestled next to me on the couch. I gave her a quick peck on the lips.

"So, how are things at your apartment?" I asked.

"About the same. Alexa and my mom are still on each other's ass, and they're turning the place into a sty."

"Are they mad at you for staying over here?"

"No, not at all. They like you. Just so I keep paying my share of the rent, they'll be fine."

"You know, why don't you bring some of your clothes over here so you don't have to run over there every day? I'd even pay your share of the rent for you."

She raised her right eyebrow in a gesture that could've been construed as anger, but it was more a signal of her resolve to earn her keep. "You don't have to pay my rent.

Just make sure I have enough for groceries." She panned her head from one end of the narrow living room to the other. "You're going to give me some space here?"

From experience, I knew this is the way cohabitation was initiated. One drawer, then two, then the bathroom, then the kitchen, then wall hangings and so on. I wanted Sophia close to me, the genuine intimate feeling was trying to unsettle my emotions, but I conceded fully.

"Sure, you can have as many drawers as you want—and half the closet," I said.

"Are you asking me to move in?"

"Well, as long as you're going to be here for at least fifty more nights, I think logistically it'd be wise for you to bring some clothes over. I mean, you've been packing up your toothbrush and toiletries every day, only to bring them back at night."

"You think you're up for that? Being newly disengaged and all to Pamela."

"You know, that seems like a lifetime ago. It's weird. It's almost like it never happened. But as far as being 'up for it,' there are some things I'd like to tell you. Things I've gone through."

Sophia hesitated. The upward cast of her eyes informed me she was calculating her words. "You don't have to tell me any deep dark secrets, but I have noticed some things about you," she said.

"I know you probably have."

Sophia directed her glance to the small dining area. "Did you see the ironing board is missing?"

I looked and noticed the middle of the room was empty. "Where is it?" I asked.

"It's safely tucked away in the hall closet. You work on the docks wearing jeans and a company shirt. Why do you compulsively iron all your clothes?"

"I don't know why. I guess I just feel more secure and relaxed with nicely pressed clothes."

Sophia smiled. "Well, I'll help you relax without having the most unwrinkled clothes in the world. I won't pass any judgment on you if your boxer shorts have a couple of wrinkles in them."

"Okay, thanks. I guess that habit has got a little out of hand."

"Like I said, I don't need to know all your secrets, but I would like to know what's going on with the medication."

"The medication *is* my dark secret." I paused and folded my arms. "As you've probably figured out, my mental state is sometimes unstable, not in a dangerous way to the outside world; there are just rickety episodes that affect me greatly. You've seen it happen to me a couple of times. But since being with you steadily, my anxiety seems to be receding. Just recently, I can live a normal life around town—go to work, eat at a restaurant, wait in line in a grocery store, get stuck in traffic. It's just traveling… I can't travel very far away from home or else I start freaking out."

"How far can you travel?"

"I don't know. Sometimes it's twenty miles, other times I can go fifty, maybe a hundred miles. It's real tough though. I wouldn't be able to drive alone much past that."

"What would happen if you did?"

"I've tried it. I just turn around and head back to safety."

Sophia's expression remained neutral. "So, that's your sordid little secret, you don't like to travel?"

"It's more than that. Traveling is very important to me. I've been all over the world and it's so frustrating—"

"Shhhh," Sophia gestured and put her index finger to my lips. "I've spent my whole life in San Pedro and haven't been any farther than Tijuana. And I've always thought I would be here all my life. If that turns out to be the case, then I want to be with someone I love truly and enjoy—and who loves their life with me."

"I don't understand," I said. "Are you talking about love?"

"Loving you? Yes," she said. "So much so that I'll make you a deal. Take me places where I've never been. I don't care where we go, or how far away. If there are problems, I'll get you back safe and secure."

"I can probably take you some places, maybe Santa Barbara or Palm Springs, but I don't think I can take you flying anywhere."

"I don't care about flying," Sophia stated as if discussing the least important issue in the world. "I've never even been on a plane. Let's just drive somewhere… anywhere. There's one stipulation, though."

My eyes widened as my heart pumped a couple of rapid, accentuated beats. "What's that?"

"You do it without medication. I've never taken a drug in my adult life—prescription or otherwise. That medicine is dragging you down."

"I don't know if I can do that."

She registered the onrushing terror enveloping my face before continuing. "I promise you'll be safe. I'll take care of you. Before you know it, you won't even dwell on the pills, and I bet you'll feel better than you think."

"We can go somewhere close, but I don't know how I'd feel without the medication. I carry some with me all the time."

"Okay, then I'll compromise. I'll carry your pills with me. Would that make you feel more secure?"

"That would be better. I just have to wean the dosages for the next week."

"I'll be your nurse."

"Will you be a nasty nurse?"

She moved her lips close until they lightly tickled my right ear. "The nastiest," she whispered.

"Awesome!"

"Then it's settled," she said. "This is the most I can give you. I don't have any material things."

"This is more than anyone outside my family has ever given me."

"I can always give you hope, that's the easy part."

"Let's go get your stuff," I said.

We drove to Sophia's apartment and I waited in the car while she got her things. The move was obviously a simple one. All she owned were three pairs of jeans, five pairs of tight bicycling shorts, five pairs of thong underwear, a few bras, a handful of t-shirts, and a pair of high-top tennis shoes. Except for a couple of knick-knacks and her car, that was about it. It was not Sophia's nature to need much. She was used to surviving in sparse materialistic surroundings for much of her life. We returned to my apartment and she gathered her things to bring inside.

"Are you sure you want to do this?" I asked as I opened the front door.

She grinned and adjusted the bundle of clothing tucked under her right arm. "I'm sure. How else could we honor our seventy night pact?" As she made her way to the bedroom, she stopped and lifted her left arm in the air, her finger pointing upward. "Wait, I forgot something. Before I put these clothes away and move in officially, I have one question for you."

Sophia returned to the living room and set her clothes on the coffee table. She curled her finger in a back and forth gesture, summoning me to follow her into the bedroom. She opened the middle drawer of the dresser and dug under my folded t-shirts. A pair of red panties appeared in her hand.

"Do you wear these often?" she asked, twirling the underwear in front of me.

I stared at Colleen's silk panties waving in front of my face. "Um, those were a gift from my neighbor in Arizona."

"Come here," Sophia said.

I followed her into the bathroom. She wadded the panties in her fist and dropped the frilly red silk ball in the toilet. She smiled and looked at me as the underwear started darkening as it soaked up the water. "You do the honors," she said, then guided her eyes downward to the flusher handle.

I pushed my finger on the flusher. We unceremoniously watched the red bundle make a swirly disappearance into the toilet abyss.

"There, that seems to take care of unwanted business," Sophia said. "Now I can put my clothes away."

20. The Canyon

The only perceptible sound I registered was the muffled whine of the cable as we ascended the canyon on the side of San Jacinto Mountain. On our third weekend outing, I got bold and decided Sophia and I would take the Palm Springs Tramway to the mountains that rose above the desert. The first weekend trip was to Ojai, a little town nestled inland from Santa Barbara, about ninety miles north from our home. The second weekend we went south to Temecula and visited a few wineries. Those trips were safely accomplished, my car always tethered nearby in case I wanted to escape. Agoraphobic thoughts poked into my head a few times, but Sophia never let it materialize to anything critical.

The Palm Springs tram was more of a challenge. I was stuck in a rotating car suspended hundreds of feet off the ground with strangers and no way to escape. It started feeling like a plane ride as we slithered up the cable away from the tram station situated in the steep Chino Canyon.

"I think I'm having a panic attack," I whispered to Sophia.

"Remember, it's just your body chemistry changing. Your carbon dioxide and oxygen levels are adjusting. It's a normal occurrence. It's happening in my body also, but I'm just not having the same reactions."

I didn't want to believe the bodily realities. "No, I think I'm experiencing difficulties. My breathing is getting shallow. It may be the altitude."

"Your tie is probably too tight," Sophia said. She loosened the tie from my collar and unfastened the top button of my dress shirt. "You don't need to wear a tie for the tram ride."

"I just wanted to look nice," I said.

"No, I think you just wanted to look unthreatening and as normal as possible in case you needed help or had an outburst with a panic attack."

I turned my head in embarrassment. "You learn fast, it's kind of degrading. But I still feel my lungs clamping from the altitude."

Sophia unfolded a piece of paper from her backpack and read some specifications. "We just passed the first tower, the highest of the five support towers at two hundred twenty-seven feet. We're almost—"

"We're two hundred twenty-seven feet above ground here?" I asked as I saw the base station get smaller in the distance and the ground falling below.

Sophia remained calm. "What I was saying is we've already traveled over a fifth of the way up the mountain." She smiled. "The ride is practically over."

I tensed my right arm and lifted it to read my digital watch. It was set on the stopwatch so I could see how much time we had left. The attendant at the station told us that the ride was a mere fifteen minutes, if there were no problems. Sophia wouldn't allow him to elaborate on what could possibly hold up the tram ride, but over three minutes had already elapsed, leaving only a dozen or so agonizing minutes left of suspension.

"How long until the next tower?" I asked.

Sophia consulted the technical specification sheet she had obtained prior to the trip. It made me feel more comfortable to break the larger excursion into smaller segments, getting through the steps one at a time. A fifteen minute tram ride to me was comparable to an overseas journey.

"It's thirty-two hundred feet between Tower One and Tower Two. Look up in front. You can see the second tower." She shifted her eyes over to mine. "We're almost forty percent of the way there… already."

"How high up are we going to go?"

With patience, Sophia consulted her spec sheet. "The elevation at the mountain station is eight thousand five hundred sixteen feet."

"That's high," I said, narrowing my eyes as I spoke. "The air may be too thin up there for me to breathe."

"Do you think that eighty-something-year-old lady over there is worried about thin air?" Sophia asked rhetorically, pointing to an elderly woman on the other side of the tram. "There's no need to worry my Sweet, the air will be crisp and robust at the end of the ride."

There was not a wavering of fear in her eyes, nor on the faces of any other passengers in the tram. It embarrassed me to make Sophia cite figures on a short tourist tram ride. I finally looked out the window to take in some scenery as we glided upward. The vertical canyon walls looked like lined granite with some vegetation outcroppings. The walls rose to pointed peaks, one after the other. It was beautiful, though I was concerned with how much farther we had to go and if the air would be breathable at the top of the mountain. I looked up at the tram's roof. With its eight-foot ceiling, I was initially worried about being enclosed with a ceiling comparable to mid-century tract homes. But Sophia got me in there, and now instead of enjoying the scenery, I consumed myself in a phobic wonderland. I looked around the car as riders young and old were intently fixed on the wonders outside the windows, captivated by the nature and awesome scope of the San Jacinto Mountains that were a blink away from the irrigated aridness of the Palm Springs area and Coachella Valley. The view was amazing; I tried to see it that way, if only my mind would let me. Instead of absorbing the incredible mountainous terrain, I thought about how glad I was that we went on the earliest tram ride. We were the first group up the mountain at eight in the morning. Even though rides commenced about every thirty minutes, I wanted to be on the first one because I surmised it would be less crowded in the early morning. The tram had a capacity of eighty people, but I counted only twenty on the ride. All that extra body space made me feel a little less apprehensive, and I believed it would be less painful if I were to embarrass myself in front of a smaller crowd. My anticipatory visions were not based on logic, though my brain plotted scenarios without ceasing—it was illogical thought logically contrived and I prayed the plots would not win over the reality.

As the tram car slowed a bit and bumped through another tower, Sophia said, "We've gone about seventy-five hundred feet, about sixty percent of the way there." She gave me a kiss on my dry lips. "You're doing real good."

"When did we pass the third tower?" I asked.

"When you were chewing your lower lip thinking about something."

I noticed during our ascent that the round tram car had rotated, taking us slowly from the back of the car to the front, offering riders a 360-degree experience. "How fast does this thing rotate?" I asked.

Once again, Sophia consulted her fact sheet. "It says here it rotates six millimeters per second."

"Six millimeters? How much is that in inches?"

She dropped the sheet into her small backpack and gave me a one-eyebrow-raised look. "I didn't bring along a conversion table with me and don't have an app on my phone. I'll have to remember to download one next time. Don't worry though, it's a very slow rotation."

"Do you have my medication?" I asked as I looked down at her backpack.

She lifted two pill bottles in her right hand and gently shook them a couple of times.

"Sorry," I said. "I'm just defraying the nerves."

"That's okay. What we are doing is 'desensitization.' You're facing your fears head-on. It's a normal way of dealing with panic attacks and agoraphobia. You'll do just fine."

"You're talking about oxygen levels in my body and medically accepted recovery terms. Are you going psychiatrist on me?" I asked.

"Maybe. But I bet you never slept with any of your psychiatrists."

"They were all men, so... no, I haven't."

"Well if you're a good patient, you will tonight," she said.

As we passed the last tower, Sophia's eyes widened. "Look, we're almost to the end."

I had the feeling then that I was indeed going to make the ascent without incident. It was now time to start churning my stomach for the ride down, that's the way the routine always panned out. The tram rocked gently and the door opened to let the passengers out.

Outside of the tram I sensed the wilderness setting while a cool forty-degree breeze infiltrated my white dress shirt that I usually reserved for wear as part of a suit outfit. The air was crisp, the green trees were beautiful. I just couldn't enjoy the atmosphere, too many negative influences were racing in my mind as we entered the mountain station.

"There's a restaurant up here. Would you like to stop for a while or just go back down?" Sophia asked.

"Let's just take this one back down when it gets turned around," I said.

"No nature for you?"

"No, sorry."

Sophia smiled. "That's okay. I'm proud you made it up here. We'll just have to wait a few minutes before the tram goes back down."

I stood looking down the steep mountain where the Palm Springs area washed out from the bottom of the canyon like an ethological alluvial fan. In the middle of the scene was the large runaway of the Palm Springs airport. I was merely riding in this little tram traveling a couple of miles up Mount San Jacinto. We were only eighty-five hundred feet in the sky, four times lower than the cruising altitude of commercial airliners. My options weighed, it made me feel a lot more secure being on this trifling mountain jaunt instead of strapped to a seat on an airplane. It made the trip a bit easier, especially since I knew we were going back down the mountain in a couple of minutes.

"It's really nice of you to take me up here. Thank you," I said. I felt like my eyes were going to water.

Sophia looked up from the map she was studying and smiled. "I'm having fun, you don't have to thank me."

"That's just it, you're doing this for me, yet having fun doing it." Tears broke loose and I fervently wiped them. I noticed the tram had made its half circle trip and was ready to go back down the mountain. The attendant was standing by the door awaiting fresh passengers. We walked to the other side of the platform to reboard the tram.

"It looks like we're going to be the only people on this ride," Sophia said as we entered the tram.

I scanned the inside of the tram and noticed that nobody else was in there except us. My brief sobbing stopped as I became weary knowing we were locked in and committed to the ride down. I walked to the front and waited.

"We're moving," Sophia said. "You see, it'll be all right. I'm here next to you, no one else is around. It's like our own personal shuttle."

Sophia went back to studying the map as I gazed out a side window with my hands firmly gripped on a safety rail. We bumped through the first two support towers in silence. The ride down seemed faster, but my breathing started getting noticeably shallow. It was in proximity to the midpoint anxiety phase of the journey--same distance going back up as it was to the end of the descent. No shorter escape route. My exhalations started producing a subtle wheezing sound. Sophia's attention was directed out an opposite window, but she suddenly turned to face me after a particularly loud breath.

"Where's San Gorgonio Mountain?" she asked.

I walked over to the other side of the tram and stood next to her. "It's north on the other side of the pass." I gulped a deep breath. "You can't see it right now; it's blocked by the side of the cliff. I climbed it once when I was a kid."

Sophia studied me intently for a moment. "You climbed San Gorgonio? How high was that?"

"About eleven thousand five hundred as I remember. It was mostly on paths, no ice picks or oxygen masks needed."

She studied me again. I wondered what she was thinking, but I didn't want to ask, my sole goal was to make it down the mountain. Sophia looked out again at the craggy cliffs off in the distance and stood silent for a minute. We had already passed the third set of support grids.

"Gorgonio is kind of an odd name," Sophia said. "Sounds like some kind of cheese served at a fancy party."

I glanced at her with a somewhat smug look on my face. I tried to pull off the aura of knowledge without revealing the inner terror that still enveloped me within the confines of the tram. "I actually know who that is named after," I said.

"Who?"

"Well, it is supposedly named after Saint Gorgonius." I nodded my head as if trying to convince her. "He was a martyr who was tortured to death in the persecution of Christians during the latter years of the Roman Empire."

"A martyr," Sophia noted.

"Yeah, he was. Saint Gorgonius was killed during the reign of Diocletian, a Roman pagan. He forbid Christians from assembling for worship and even made some of them torture their own people or face death themselves."

Sophia's focus was still concentrated on me. "Who was this Diocletian guy?"

"He was the emperor who divided the Roman Empire into two main empires."

"And why did he do that?" Sophia asked immediately.

"I guess it was from all the civil wars breaking out within the Empire. It became too cumbersome to keep peace and defend the land. Basically, he divided East and West, with emperors appointed to rule the divided areas."

Sophia widened her eyes a bit in amusement. "And you know all of this how?"

"I… guess I took a lot of history classes as electives in college. Sorry, my long-term memory is still intact."

The tram had rotated enough to give us a view from the back. I noticed the slowing of our movement as we glided through another support tower. The surroundings outside the tram had a more arid appearance, thin sprigs of vegetation outcropped from the rocky canyon walls.

"We're heading for the last tower," Sophia said. "Your dissertation on the Romans kept your mind off the ride--for at least a tower segment." Her mouth crooked a one-sided grin, knowing that I knew I was probably going to make the whole ride without incident.

I nodded my head, now realizing why she was looking at me so keenly during my history critique. "So… you were just keeping me talking."

"No, simply getting you down a mountain."

Sophia put her arm around me while I stared out the window and noticed our descent had flattened a few degrees. We were almost at the lower tram station, the end of the line. I glanced down at my wrist and noticed that I hadn't even reset my stopwatch for the second leg of the journey.

After the tram had come to a stop, Sophia grabbed my hand and led me through the station. I welcomed the solid ground though my feelings were very subtle, as if a normal person taking the ride. No real relief, just the ordinariness of enjoying a diversion before going on to the next errand.

"What do you want to do now?" I asked.

"Well, it's not even nine in the morning, but I've got a craving." Sophia kissed me on my cheek. "Let's go find a place to stay tonight, but we can take a little nap in the late morning."

"Oh, I think I get it. What's the big turn-on? Tram rides make you horny?"

"I just want to sleep with one of my patients," Sophia teased. "You've never slept with any of your psychiatrists, and I don't want you to feel deprived."

"Sounds like a great plan. Where would you like this forbidden relationship to take place?"

Sophia put her index finger to her cheek and slowly rotated her head to view the Palm Springs area that folded out in front of us.

"Any ideas?" I asked.

"Your choice. Anywhere but places in this town you've happencd to spend with other women."

I smiled. "No problem, can rule out a few places, but still plenty of options. Let's go, Doc."

21. Taking Care

Over the next six weeks, Sophia and I continued our weekend excursions. I would plan our destination and route during the week. Every Friday, we forged through the evening rush hour traffic to wend our way outside the Los Angeles area.

"Did you bring my medication?" I kept asking on the first few journeys.

Sophia would casually reach into the back seat, open her backpack, and reveal two small bottles of medication, one containing Xanax, the other Nardil. I never took any while on the trips, but it made me feel safer having them near in case I needed some pharmaceutical comforting.

With every new outing, my agoraphobia steadily cleared as my geographical prison expanded farther from my safety zone. We went to Las Vegas for a long weekend, took a drive up the coast to Carmel and the Monterey Peninsula, and even camped under the stars near Yosemite. Sophia would busy herself during the extended drives by reading books and online articles on panic disorder and psychology. With every new trip, the back seat held larger stacks of books and articles. She was amassing a small medical library.

Every place we went was a new experience for her. It was as if we were grown kids going out in the world for the first time. Ironically, my boundaries had shrunk extensively from past intercontinental travels, while Sophia was just beginning to broaden her borders. These short trips were monumental to both of us for totally different reasons. I was just happy to be able to travel even a hundred miles. Sophia enjoyed the exposure to new places and my ailment was genuinely an interesting study for her.

As our drives logged multiple hours and hundreds of miles, I felt an unmistakable comfort in her presence. No need to hide anything—a considerable amount of psychical weight had lifted off my shoulders.

"I think I've found my true calling," she revealed while we carted north through the Central Valley one weekend on I-5. "Finding wayward men to help."

"I have to say you do take care of me. I don't understand why some guy didn't swoop you up long ago."

"It probably could've happened. I was just waiting for some neurotic jerk to come along."

I stiffened, weighing the accuracy of her statement. I looked at Sophia and she started laughing, flushing away my apprehension. It could have been her old-world Greek roots that made her so tough yet nurturing, or a bit of Hispanic blended in from a bygone generation. My parents came to know of Sophia as an acquaintance of mine in the weeks that followed, but I never discussed our budding accord. Given my past track record, I tried to keep our relationship as low profile as I could—especially since I was engaged to Pamela only a short time ago.

With each succeeding weekend, my panic symptoms gradually abated. Sophia herself encountered only one complication during a visit to Devils Postpile on the slopes of the Sierra Nevada near Mammoth Mountain, a popular skiing destination for people from Southern California. As we made our way up the eastern slope of the Sierra Nevada above the Owens Valley on U.S Highway 395, Sophia doubled over in pain suddenly.

"My stomach really hurts," she grunted.

"Let me take you to a hospital," I said. Panic tried to rear its head but was held at bay by the crisis at hand.

"No, that's okay. But do you mind if we delay going to Devils Postpile for a few hours? Maybe we can rest at a hotel."

"Of course not. We can even go back home. We're about six hours away."

"No, just go to a hotel. I'll be fine in a while."

I turned the car around and headed back to the town of Bishop. I found an old ranch-style motel just off the highway. As soon as we got into the room, Sophia dashed to the bathroom. "I've got to throw up," she said while closing the door.

I went to an all-night convenience store and bought two small cartons of orange juice and a pack of energy bars. During the drive, my concern for her trumped any possible agoraphobia that tended to swirl in my thoughts. It just wasn't there. No initial pumping heartbeat, no skewed perception of being in reality, no fear of being detached. When I returned to the room, Sophia was stretched out across the bed.

"My stomach feels swollen. And it hurts. Maybe it's food poisoning."

"Rest, Honey. We don't have to go to Devils Postpile."

"We will go," Sophia insisted in a voice that was overtly labored. "Just give me a few hours and I'll be ready."

"We'll see. I have some orange juice and snacks if you want any."

"I'll take some juice," she said.

I cupped my hand behind her head and tipped the juice carton to her mouth. Her straight hair slipped softly in my palm as she situated her head to take the first sip. After tending to her few sips, I removed my clothing and threw my pants and shirt next to the TV before I snuggled next to her on the bed.

* * * *

"I'm ready, let's go." Sophia's voice brought me out of a deep sleep.

My eyes opened and I saw unfamiliar surroundings. It took a second to remember we were in a cheap motel in Bishop.

"You're ready to go where?"

"To Devils Postpile. Come on, get up."

"How long did we sleep?"

"About five hours. But we need to get going."

I slid out of bed and looked around the room for my clothes. Sometime during my slumber, Sophia had neatly folded and placed them on the chair by the front window.

"How do you feel?" I asked.

"I'm fine. Get some clothes on that sexy body of yours."

While I slipped my clothes on, Sophia went outside and stood by the car. As I went out the hotel door, she was wrapping her red bandana around her hair. I froze for a moment to admire her before approaching the car. We jumped in and drove off without bothering to check out of the place.

Sophia sat quietly while we traversed up the mountain on Route 395 to Devils Postpile. The last seven miles of the drive was on a narrow, bumpy road off the main highway. Although Sophia seemed run down, her stoic will to conclude the trip was stronger than her fatigue and lingering pain.

Devils Postpile was a spectacular formation of sixty-foot high columnar basalt created from lava flow that once filled the mountain valley. We hiked up to the towering columns of Devils Postpile with the serene fluid flow of the nearby San Joaquin River serving as a soothing audible background setting. We found another trail leading to the top of the formation. Sophia labored as we climbed the steep incline. She never complained, never stopped. Once there, we stood and marveled at the basalt columns. Large columnar pieces had fallen below the formation, giving the illusion of standing above ancient Greek ruins. I stared at the natural wonder and couldn't help feeling a pang of contentment from another successful trip, though I was concerned about Sophia's stomachache. She didn't let on that it was still hurting, but I could see soreness in her posture—a slight hunch coupled with a tentative stride.

Sophia slept most of the way on the drive home. I was once again on a desolate high desert road with miles separating small towns. There was no discomfort on the drive, as if I had forgotten all the hours that I had spent on isolated highways slipping into mental breakdowns. Though Sophia was next to me, my confidence had grown to the point of believing I could actually be on the drive alone and suffer no panic. The past started to seem no longer relevant as the present had incremental breakthroughs of optimism. The brain works in strange ways: Conditionable, yet still a tough customer.

When we arrived at the apartment late that evening, Sophia hugged me tightly as we walked in the door.

"You took good care of me when I was sick," she said.

The thought hadn't entered my mind prior, but it gave me a tinge of pride being able to help her for even a short moment of time, when the relationship had been, since the beginning, her taking care of me. As Sophia gave me one last tight squeeze to end the hug, I came to recognize that ours was a peculiar union, the sheltered beauty hooking up with a philandering agoraphobe—an odd couple that seemed to fit in its own trivial way.

Though flying was still something I could not even think of doing, the heartache of staying on the ground seemed to ebb as I concentrated more on my immediate traveling victories. I even called Dr. Crouch's office to cancel future appointments. Sophia seemed to do more for me than any doctor I'd ever consulted. My panic along with the myriad of offshoot ailments were almost becoming manageable. The cycle of depression had been broken. After leaving the message with Dr. Crouch's secretary, I knew he wouldn't call me back. He was now just the guy who gave me a tip on body mulch and filled prescriptions that I no longer took. I wouldn't change his life or schedule at all, he'd just fill my appointment slot with the next hapless patient who came along--and there were always new poor suckers evolving daily.

22. The Fall

"Where are we going this weekend?" Sophia rolled over and asked as I woke up to greet an August Thursday morning.

"Catalina Island," I said.

"A boat? You think you can handle that?"

"I love boats, it's being detached from land that gets me. But no problem, I can handle the ferry ride. It's what, maybe two hours? Piece of cake."

Sophia gave me a kiss, then pulled back in surprise. "It's our seventieth night together," she exclaimed.

"It is?" I rotated my head, scanning the bedroom. "Does that mean you're going to gather your clothes and leave?"

She nodded her head casually. "No, I think I'll stick around."

"That's cause for a little celebration."

With a mischievous grin, I wiggled my body under the silky bed sheet to inspect her naked flesh. Her legs slid open wide enough for me to nuzzle myself between, working my way to the small soft tuft of shiny dark hair between her legs.

Her hips swayed as my tongue moved across her. I stroked my hands over her front, surrounding her bellybutton with my fingers. My kneading hands registered her stomach jutting outward in an exaggerated slope. The rise began two inches below her belly button, cresting at the middle of her abdomen.

As I continued enjoying Sophia, I couldn't help but direct my eyes at her protruding stomach as her back arched up and down. I pushed my hands over the area again, noticing it was firm, almost rock hard. It felt like there was part of an upside-down bowl affixed under her skin.

I had detected a slight bloat to her stomach when she was sick on our trip to Devils Postpile, but I'd hoped it was nothing more than an intestinal bug. Now with my head nestled between her legs, the lower vantage point revealed a lump that had grown to an unmistakably round, compacted mass. Her waist was still as skinny as when we met, and her body didn't appear any heavier. It was as if a ball had been sewn underneath her skin while the rest of her remained untouched. After a few minutes, Sophia stiffened her long legs and moaned loudly.

Still focused on her abdomen, my concern overshadowed the exhilaration of giving her pleasure. I knew by now I could talk about anything with Sophia, but I was lost on how to approach the subject of her distended stomach.

I had never knowingly knocked up a girl and was ignorant as to the speed with which a woman's belly grew while carrying a child. Her midsection had the bulged appearance of early pregnancy, creating an instant pang of fear within me. Not that I didn't want children, I just worried about being able to support them if my panic disorder ever disabled me completely. It was never the fear of kids, it was the uncertainty of myself. But Sophia and I had discussed this subject during our drives, and I learned she was all for having kids and she thought I would make a great father, no matter my condition. Bearing her beliefs in mind, there was no sense pondering how to ask her.

"You know, your stomach is really round and hard." I glided my hand over the area.

"I know," she said, self-consciously turning on her side.

"You were sick when we were at that motel in Bishop. Are you pregnant?"

"No."

"It's not natural to have a growing lump in your stomach."

She ran her fingers across her abdomen. "I think it started about a year ago when I fell off a wall."

"A wall?"

"I was at a punk concert sitting on a wall to the side of the stage. Someone pushed me, and I fell."

"How high?" I asked.

"About eight feet, I guess. I landed right on my side. It hurt for a couple of weeks, then kind of stopped."

"Did you ever have that checked out?"

"No."

"This could be internal bleeding or something. When's the last time you saw a doctor?"

"I saw a gynecologist six years ago. That's the last time I went to a doctor. It's been hurting lately. Not my stomach, it feels more like my intestines are shifting."

"Yeah, I bet. Promise me you'll get that checked out as soon as possible. I don't want anything to be wrong with you."

"I don't have any insurance. Even if I did, the deductible would be too high. But I can go to Harbor General and see a doctor—that's what some of my friends do."

"Just do it," I said firmly. "Don't be scared to see a doctor. I'll pay for it if you need me to. It's probably nothing, but should be examined."

23. Fashionably Late

The alarm rang at half past five. My right arm floated automatically atop the "off" switch to subdue the intrusion. I noticed a wicked adrenaline rush in me, one that not too long ago was an acutely familiar companion. The feeling failed to cause heightened concern because I knew this was the beginning of no ordinary day.

I stared at Sophia. She looked so beautiful on the bed. I loved the way her long hair fell over her body and flowed on to me. Many times we would fall asleep clutching each other and could remain that way until morning.

One minute after I stifled the alarm, Sophia arose and got to work preparing for the unknown. She put on her skintight black bicycle pants and an old t-shirt from my failed auto detailing business. I hoped she would fare better than the business did.

It was getting lighter outside as Sophia switched lights off and on, nervously preparing for her trip to the hospital. I staggered over to the dresser and pulled a pair of unironed, but acceptably wrinkleless shorts over my naked body. I didn't need to get ready for work just yet. In fact, as I adjusted the cotton shorts around my waist, I could tell by the tingling feeling in my gut that I wasn't quite ready for the entire day.

Just fifteen days after Sophia saw a doctor for her hardened stomach, she was scheduled for surgery. Her appointment turned out to be anything but routine as multiple specialists at Harbor-UCLA Medical Center viewed the ultrasound of Sophia's insides.

The protrusion turned out to be a large tumor growing inside her... and it had nothing to do with falling off a wall a year earlier. The doctors decided removing and analyzing the mass was of vital importance. At first they planned to obtain a small sample for a biopsy, but due to its abnormal size, they elected to operate as soon as their schedules allowed.

There was not much conversation between us as she brushed her black hair methodically, from the top of her scalp all the way down to the ends just above her rear. She originally wanted to pull her hair into a ponytail with her lucky red bandana, but worried the bandana may get misplaced at the hospital. As she scurried around the apartment, I wished I had an idea of what was going through her mind. I could tell she was edgy, though I didn't quite know how to calm her.

"I wanted to drive you to the hospital."

"I know, but my mom insisted."

"You're going to be all right."

"I just wish I knew what they're going to do to me," she said, tensing the inner edges of her dark eyebrows closer together.

"Well, the doctors went over all of that in your preliminary appointment. They're going to put you under and pull that thing out of you. Then sew you up and I'll take care of you from there." I added a quick peck on her cheek to soften the abridged clinical utterance.

A moment later, her mom's car horn honked from Capital Avenue as morning commuters whizzed by.

"I love you," Sophia said. Her body felt rigid as I hugged her tightly. I could sense the fear in her frame.

"I love you too. You'll be all right." As she pulled away from our embrace, I noticed one tear coming from each eye. "Don't cry, you'll do just fine and I'll see you tonight."

"You don't even know what room I'll be in."

"I'll find you."

I watched her walk with stiff strides to her mother's old faded Cadillac. She went through a rarely used unlocked gate off the sidewalk that led out to the street. When the car door creaked opened, I heard Barbara Syros apologizing frantically for being late. Her arms flailed about, helping her enunciate the words. They drove off leaving me standing by the doorway wearing only knee-length shorts. I wondered if indeed this was going to be a routine operation.

* * * *

I stopped to purchase a dozen red roses after work and drove through the cities of Lomita and Torrance, eventually entering Harbor City. Harbor General, as it was known, or even just Harbor to locals, was a sizable county hospital catering to mainly welfare and economically poor patients. Harbor's parking lot was a huge slab of concrete and asphalt that seemingly stretched about five blocks behind the main building. The hospital's original architecture was late 1940s utilitarian vintage. The exterior surfaces had undergone a facelift within the past decade, giving the structure a more updated covering—though it was still a cold and sterile looking place.

Not knowing exactly where to go after parking my car, I entered the first door I saw. It whisked me into the emergency room waiting area. The large room was a disturbing mass of people, most bearing withered drawn faces. I passed crying babies, patients with wounded appendages clutching bloody rags, coughers, wheezers, snifflers and the terminally waiting bored. The open room, about the size of a modest conference center, appeared almost Third World in its human despair. The bunch of red roses in my hand was the only pleasant thing in the area. I dashed through a pair of oversized swinging doors located on the far side of the ER. My feet seemed to lead me automatically as I made a left turn down a corridor and spotted a nurse's station.

"Spelled S-I-R?" the slender brunette nurse asked.

"No, S-Y-R," I said.

She consulted a sheet on a clipboard. "She's in the recovery room, but is assigned to room 308, upstairs."

As the sliding elevator door revealed the third floor, I noticed the stark linoleum walkways and an overall disinfected atmosphere that didn't leave much to the eye. Familiar faces appeared as I stepped out of the elevator. A buzz stirred around a small waiting area to my right as news of my arrival traveled. Sophia's mom walked to me hunched over as if cinderblocks were affixed to her back.

"Where have you been?" Barbara Syros asked in desperation, abruptly wiping the smile off my face.

"I stopped after work to get some flowers," I said. "The nurse told me she's still in the recovery room."

"Where were you?" she repeated, clutching a moist well-used tissue in her left hand. Her sad eyes revealed evidence of heavy crying. "We called, but you didn't answer. Sophia wanted you to be here, she loves you."

I pulled my cell phone out of my pocket and realized it had turned off sometime in the past couple of hours. My mood went from a suitor bearing flowers for his ailing love, to a dread that left me instantly flushed.

"Is she okay?"

Barbara looked at me dumbfounded as tears flowed out of her puffy eyes. "Sophia has cancer all over. You weren't here when the doctor told us an hour ago. No, she's not well." Barbara's eyes grew more intense with desperation as she gave the diagnosis. "She has cancer."

The word "cancer" didn't immediately register. My instincts led me to comfort Barbara instead of hearing the true words—what that meant for Sophia, what it meant for us, what it meant for me. I gave Barbara a hug. She sobbed, her soft body trembling in my arms.

A dozen of Sophia's family members were in the small waiting area. Everyone was glad to see I had finally arrived, this magic man of Sophia's whom they had heard so much about. I had met two of her aunts and one uncle at a Syros family barbecue Sophia and I attended about two months ago. The other visitors were new faces except for Alexa and Rosa, who were sitting solemnly on brown plastic chairs that lined the back wall of the small waiting area. As I met them one by one, they all expressed how glad they were Sophia was with somebody who cared about her. Her life had not been the most auspicious one on record, so an educated guy from the right upbringing appeared to her family as a fortunate turn of events—no matter my mental incontinence.

The lugubrious aura overflowed in the immediate area as I sat on one of the plastic chairs and waited for Sophia's release from the recovery room. Her relatives were searching for answers as to why a twenty-eight-year-old woman would be stricken with cancer. They were all very devout Catholics and truly believed that it was *God's will*, and now her cure rested in higher hands.

I was not from an overly religious upbringing. Not because my family wasn't religious, rather we were just too busy when I was younger to attend church regularly. I stayed out of discussing the religious doctrine Sophia's family held with great conviction as a cure for her disease. My belief rested more on some higher source laying a card on the table, and it came up cancer. If her condition turned out to be mortal, God wouldn't cure her. The only thing God could cure Sophia of… was virulent life itself.

Life Unbothered — Charlie Elliott

As I sat slumped over staring at the floor, a stout yet feminine hand slowly rubbed the top of my shoulder.

"I'm so glad Sophia has you," said Beatrice, the more grandmotherly of Sophia's two aunts. I pulled my head up to view her friendly round face. Her thick glasses magnified the size of her eyes, making her appear a bit overzealous at first sight, but she had a comforting smile that overshadowed the optics of her enlarged orbs.

"Yes, she is so lucky to have found you, Wade," the younger Aunt Marlene swooned in a loving voice as I resumed my floor staring.

I noticed the space around the chair filled quickly as five pairs of middle-aged feet appeared on the linoleum. I glanced up to see five women standing over me, each of them revealing strained smiles.

"Oh Wade will take care of her," came in from my right side.

"You will take care of her, won't you?" came in from my left.

All five women nodded affirmatively in unison, which left me with only one uneasy answer, "Yes… of course I'll take care of her." The ladies had made short work of negotiating and hammering out an oral contract with me.

I continued sitting on the chair with my hand cupped around my chin while Sophia's two aunts, her mother, and two other women I'd just met engulfed me with their gleeful smiles. A tingling sensation crept up my spine when I figured out I had just pledged to take care of Sophia. They continued gawking with a glimmer of hope in their eyes, as if I could do something for her. Glancing at each one of their gleaming faces, the scene started to make me claustrophobic. The ladies encircled me, perhaps afraid I would walk out, losing the only hope for their beloved Sophia—other than God.

Dizziness began setting in as the view of the women began warping back and forth. I imagined they were laughing and chanting one-by-one, *"Wade, you said you'd take care of her. It's all on your shoulders now. You promised."* It became evident that being a savior could come at a heavy price.

The women around me dispersed gradually, allowing the reality to sink in—Sophia had cancer. My head began to spin anew as I wondered how to handle the situation. Getting up and walking out on the whole scene did come to mind. I could concoct a story that Sophia and I were merely dating and our relationship wasn't as serious as they thought, but promise to visit her occasionally during her hopeful recovery. Or for a dramatic flair, go running down the hall screaming, "I can't take this," jump into the elevator, and disappear forever. In need of some quiet reflection, I excused myself, left the flowers on an empty chair and ducked out of the waiting area while family members continued to wait.

About fifty feet down the wide hall was a children's wing. I slipped through the swinging doors as unassumingly as possible. The wing was dead quiet and dimly lit from the few working fluorescent lights. The hospital staff was not using the area at the time and gave off a vibe of suddenly being transported to an abandoned building with all the fixtures still intact.

I shoved my hands into the front pockets of my Levis jeans and stiffened my arms, pushing hard until I heard gentle little rips in the pocket seams. Inhaling deeply, I searched for some comfort within the confines of the deserted wing as the first swirl of an anxiety tornado formed in my stomach. I wouldn't know how to cope with her having cancer. If I stayed with her, would I have to constantly take care of her and wait on her day and night? Spoon feed her and clean up drool running down her chin? My mind went into overload as my ignorance of cancer initiated different awful scenarios popping rapid-fire in my mind.

Guilt flushed over me as I pondered sel concerns about how her cancer would affect me, when I was not the one facing the dread of the diagnosis. Needing some consultation, I removed my phone from my front pocket and called my dad. He was usually much better about business matters than personal ones, but I just wanted to talk to somebody outside of Sophia's family.

"Hi, Dad." I paused, trying to stifle my emotion. "Remember I told you about Sophia's operation today? Uh… she apparently has cancer. Nobody could tell me what type of cancer yet, but by the reactions of her family, I'd presume it's not optimistic."

"Oh, that's too bad, Wade. I'm sorry to hear that," he said slowly.

"Yeah, I know. It's just very sad."

"Well, she'll probably be fine. Cancer is often treatable nowadays."

"I don't know, her mom said Sophia has cancer all over, whatever that means."

"I'm glad her mom is there and I'm sure she has many other concerned friends like you waiting for her."

"But she's more than a friend," I admitted.

My dad didn't say anything for a moment and then sighed. "Son, it's nice of you to be there, but you do not need to get wrapped up in somebody's problem right now."

My eyes bulged as I heard his response. "I'm already wrapped up in this, Dad."

"Well, as I said, it would be better to just be a good friend to her," my dad stated with steely control.

I took his comment to imply that all I should do is visit her once in a while and maybe bring some flowers or a little stuffed animal—similar to the escape plan I had envisioned earlier in the waiting room.

Just be a good friend to her? How could he say that? How callous, cold, insensitive...

"You know, I love that woman," I said with a shaky voice. "How the hell can you talk about being a good friend to her?"

There was a silent gap over the line before my dad responded. "Wade, I'm sorry. Your mom and I didn't know you two were that close. You never told us."

"Well now you know. I need to see if she's out of the recovery room. See you later." I hung up the phone before he could respond.

As my anger brewed, I was feeling pinched from Sophia's female relatives stooping over me and hammering out a convalescent commitment just a few minutes earlier. I was deferring my fear and anger to my dad even though he had no idea the extent of our relationship. I wanted to explain to my parents over a month ago that I loved Sophia, but could never muster the courage.

My body felt like it had suddenly gained about two hundred pounds as I stood in the abandoned children's wing. My posture slouched, and I felt once again, as if I weren't real. I held my hands in front of me and ducked my head to scan my body visually. I wasn't sure if I could handle what was to come, but the reaction from my father's 'friend' comment verified the right thing to do concerning Sophia. I couldn't turn my back on her, couldn't run away, couldn't get out of the situation by merely leaving the scene as I had during countless panic attacks. Despite anyone's opinion, I knew I had to take care of Sophia.

Upon returning from the children's wing, I could see Sophia's relatives gathered in front of the doorway of one of the rooms. As I walked down the aseptic hall at a reserved pace, I peered into the other rooms and noted they were just as drably decorated as every place else in the hospital. All the rooms were identical—just the humanity and tragedies were different.

"Sophia's here!" I heard an uncle declare as I approached the group. Her bed was wheeled into the room while I was having an epiphany in the children's wing. I missed the doctor's news of cancer, and now I missed Sophia arriving to her room. I was relieved no one alerted me of my absence when I walked through the door.

As I stepped into room 308, I noticed there was a sink to the right with long faucet handles. Next to the sink was a hypodermic needle disposal bin hanging on the wall with a tiny padlock affixed through a rickety hasp. Small dried blood drippings speckled randomly around the disposal slot on top of the bin. The mirror above the sink was brightly lit by a fat fluorescent tube affixed above it. As I gave myself the once-over in the mirror, the glow emanating from the light produced an exaggerated effect of facial pallor.

The room had four beds all occupied by females, two on each side of the room. The area would have been square in shape, but a small bathroom cut out one corner. There was one curtainless window extending across the back wall. Sophia was in bed number one, located on the right side of the room nearest to the door and closest to the shared bathroom.

As I wandered slowly past a few of her relatives, my eyes met Sophia's. I grabbed her left hand as I moved to the side of her reclined body. She looked somewhat comfortable, considering there was a tube coming out of her right nostril that traveled down into her abdomen for drainage, and two IVs in her arm. One IV was about a liter-sized clear bottle with a glucose solution in it, the other smaller plastic bag contained an antibiotic. Her heavy eyelids strained to stay open as the painkillers still ran through her bloodstream.

"Hi," I said.

Without moving her head, Sophia shifted her dark eyes to meet mine.

"I love you," she said in a scratchy, almost silent voice.

"I love you too," I said, feeling rather embarrassed as I glanced at all of the relatives standing around the bed. I was trying to speak in an upbeat voice instead of a drab Quaalude-type monotone—which is how I felt as the fatigue of the day was finally settling in. "I told you I'd find your room. How do you feel?"

"Okay."

I shifted my position to make space for the ladies stacking flowers on the nearby bed stand. Someone had picked up my rose bouquet from the waiting area and placed it closest to Sophia's bed.

"Do you hurt?"

"Yeah, my stomach hurts a little, but my throat really hurts right now."

"Well, you look good."

She rolled her eyes slowly. "I bet."

Barbara nudged next to my side. Her face was utterly stricken with grief. The other female relatives tucked in close, obviously wanting to talk with Sophia. I stepped back and relinquished my bedside space I had held for less than a minute. Everyone else in the room casted nervous smiles as they searched for things to say, stuff to share with Sophia. I could tell by her reactions she didn't want to talk, but it did give her some comfort knowing people were there. No one really knew how to handle the situation; I could include myself in that crowd. The relatives remained for about ten more minutes before Barbara announced that Sophia probably wanted to be alone with me. An instant later, as if choreographed, everyone filed out of the room. I addressed a general goodbye to the small crowd as they vacated.

Relieved to be alone with Sophia, my legs pressed so hard against the bed railing it felt as if blood would completely cease flowing to my feet. Her black hair stood out against the stark white bed linen as I watched her look straight ahead, seemingly staring at nothing.

"I love you," she said, breaking her fixed gaze.

"I love you too. And don't worry Honey, I'll be there for you whenever you need me."

Our hands met and I bent over the bed rail to give her a kiss on the lips, trying hard not to bump the tube snaking into her nose.

"Are you sure you still love me?" she asked with no expression. I imagined she was worried that I might indeed leave her, no longer enchanted with her cancer-stricken body. Her inherent perceptiveness led me to believe she knew the running-off plan had crossed my mind.

"I brought you the best bouquet of flowers here, didn't I? I still want to screw your lights out when I come home every night," I answered. She managed to crack a sarcastic smile and a little half-breathed laugh. "Of course I still love you."

"What's going to happen to me?"

"We'll have to wait for the doctors. I heard a nurse in the hallway say they'll be here at eight o'clock tomorrow morning. I'm not sure what kind of cancer you have or the extent of it. Your mom may know, but if so, I didn't hear. Regardless of the situation, I'll get you through this just as you got me through my fear of traveling. Many people lead productive lives after having cancer."

"Visiting hours are now over," the speaker above the door blared, then repeated the message in Spanish.

"Do you have to leave?" Sophia pleaded.

"No, don't worry about it," I said, as if I owned the hospital.

I sat quietly by the side of her bed for another two hours and didn't take my eyes off her. Draped over the white sheets, an ivory-colored blanket stretched to the top of her breasts. I scanned her covered body, wondering what was going on inside that slender frame. She drifted in and out of sleep. I stayed until she finally closed her eyes for fifteen minutes solid.

"Honey, I'm going to go now," I whispered.

Her eyes opened wide. "Okay."

I gave her a kiss and waved my tongue across the front of her teeth, wetting a portion of her parched upper lip. Her eyes closed as I moved away from the bed. I paused before going out the door to take another glance at her, then as if an automatic mechanical function, my hands drifted into the pockets of my jeans as I turned and exited to the now empty hallway at Harbor General.

24. The Diagnosis

The next morning I made my way up to room 308 at Harbor, which now seemed oddly familiar to me, though it was only my second visit. Sophia was on her bed reclined at a forty-five-degree angle. The ivory blanket lay atop her exactly as it had been when I left the night before.

As I approached to greet Sophia, a dark-haired woman clad in a white clinician's coat entered and stopped at the foot of the bed. Before I could take another step, a short man passed me and situated himself next to the woman. Both systematically raised their clipboards to scan their notes. It was straight-up eight o'clock – at least the doctors were on time.

"Good morning, I'm Dr. Hieri," the woman addressed Sophia with self-controlled sincerity.

"And I am Dr. So," the man announced as if reciting lines from a script. "I was the doctor who operated on you."

"How are you doing… Sophia?" Dr. Hieri had to refer to her clipboard in search of Sophia's name.

Dr. Hieri was an attractive Indian woman in her late thirties, with shoulder-length black hair and skin a shade lighter than most people from India I had met in my life. She spoke clearly, concealing any hint of an accent.

"Are you doing better?" Dr. Hieri asked in a slow, calculated fashion as if Sophia didn't understand English.

"Yeah. When will I be released?"

"You need to stay until we are confident your condition is conducive for release."

"She's kind of anxious to get out of here," I inserted myself into the conversation as both doctors looked at me in unison, eyeing me from head to toe.

"And you are?" Dr. Hieri asked.

"I'm Wade Hampton, her boyfriend." I extended my hand to shake hers.

"Okay, nice to meet you," Dr. Hieri said, then clasp my hand hesitantly and gave a soft handshake. She turned to Sophia and asked, "Does your boyfriend have consent to deal with this matter?"

Sophia consented with one nod of her head.

Dr. So gave me a nod of approval, but we didn't shake hands due to Dr. Hieri being in front of him, blocking our handshake path. Dr. So was a Chinese man about fifty years old. His black thick-rimmed glasses covered all of his eye socket area and half of his forehead, making his receding hairline less prominent. He was about five feet, four inches with a solid, trunkish build that fostered the presence of being stronger than his height suggested.

Dr. So tugged on the drab green divider curtain around the bed to ensure privacy and pulled opened Sophia's gown, exposing a long incision running sixteen vertical inches across the center of her body. The scalpel broke the flesh between her breasts and slid down her torso, making a curved detour around her belly button, before concluding at the top of her now shaved pubic hair. Along the laceration about every inch or so, bulky staples pierced her skin to close the wound. Heavy black stitching intertwined sparingly beneath the staples, causing the opposing sides of flesh to press against one another in a craggy raised fashion. The end result looked like a scale model of a red-walled canyon with a dried blood river running down the center of it. I tried to subdue my reaction by redirecting my attention back to Dr. So. His eyes scanned her slender midriff as he scrutinized his work.

"It seems you are recovering well from surgery," Dr. So said in a clinical manner, with a distinct but not too heavy accent.

As he moved away from the bed, a button on his white coat snagged on one of Sophia's IV tubes, producing a tugging motion on her right arm. She winced and exhaled as the needle moved in her flesh. Dr. So whisked the front of his coat to loosen the stuck button and made his way back to the foot of the bed.

"Let me go over what we found during the operation and the analysis of the tumor." Dr. So ever so slightly rolled his head over to me as to infer I was included in the discussion. "You have a mucinous cystadenocarcinoma of the ovary. We gave you a hysterectomy and removed as much mass as we could. We did not perform a colostomy as per your instructions before the surgery. We only went after the tumorous mass."

Dr. So was getting ready to speak again when I interjected.

"How large was the tumor?"

"About the size of… a volleyball," he said with no expression except for a little twinkle in his eyes, perhaps proud of his analogy any non-medical person could understand. My jaw gaped while I imagined the doctors trying to free as many pieces of that *thing* growing inside her. As I gazed at the elongated scar, Dr. Hieri draped the gown back over Sophia's uncovered body.

"In plain terms, you have ovarian cancer with metastases, meaning it has spread to other parts of your body," Dr. So said.

"Is it in her lymph system?" I asked. Not knowing a whole lot about cancer, the lymph system was one of the few ways I had heard cancer spreads throughout the body.

Dr. So shifted his eyes to mine without moving his head, "It is most likely. The tumor was analyzed in the lab last night and determined to be Stage 3C, which means it is quite advanced."

Sophia remained motionless on the bed as Dr. Hieri made the finishing adjustments to her gown.

"This tumor was caught too late. Cancer spreads fast in a young person like you," Dr. So said. "You are how old?"

"Twenty-eight," Sophia mumbled.

Dr. So produced a subtle nod of sympathy. His narrow eyes grew round beneath his thick, black-rimmed glasses as he checked off a sheet on his clipboard marking the topics reviewed.

"Your… prognosis is poor and condition viewed as terminal."

Sophia's smooth olive skin paled to a light greenish tinge. "Am I going to die?" she struggled to ask, her throat still sore from the tube running down her esophagus.

"Not necessarily. We estimated a ten percent survival rate."

Sophia's head whipped back.

"Ten percent?" I responded, as a fierce rush of blood propelled to my head. "What does that mean?"

"There is a cancer survival rate scale based on a five-year life expectancy." Dr. So began his explanation as if he were reading from a textbook. "If a person lives for more than five years after diagnosed with cancer, they are considered as having survived, or beaten cancer. We assign a percentage value on the probability a person will live more than five years. From the stage of Sophia's cancer, we believe there is a ten percent chance she will live for five years."

"So how long does she have to live?" The fear turned my voice combative. Dr. So sensed my rush of frustration yet he remained composed.

"We do not know. That is why we use percentages. There is no way to tell, in time terms, how long. It could be a month, it could be years."

"What else can we do?" I asked.

"Due to the advanced stage coupled with the financial difficulties due to lack of insurance, there is not much more we can do here at this hospital."

I stared at Dr. So, trying to keep myself from lashing out at him. "A lack of insurance, that's what this is about?"

Dr. So bowed his head slightly. "No. It has to do primarily with the terminal nature of her condition. We considered chemotherapy but decided against it solely for medical reasons, not financial reasons. Having insurance would not produce a more positive outcome in this case. Her terminal condition is best taken care of in the comfort of her own home. After she is released and we remove her stitches, we will examine her as needed."

I rolled my eyes in disbelief as both doctors headed out the door.

"We will check on you at the end of the day," Dr. Hieri said. She led the way out of the room with Dr. So behind her as they continued their rounds.

I moved up against the bed and caressed Sophia's left cheek. I felt great pain for her. Any future we could have possibly made together was halted abruptly, replaced by a dim path of uncertainty. Our hands met as I leaned over the bedrail to give her a long kiss. From the dismal diagnosis and Sophia's reaction, I knew my attitude had to change, shift over to the productive side. I now had to be strong for Sophia, instead of the other way around—the way our relationship had been up to this point.

"I don't want to die," she said.

"Then fight the cancer."

"How?" Sophia asked in a voice noticeably dusted with desperation, though she tried to hold back the emotion. "You heard the diagnosis."

Sophia was a realist at her core. A well-defined technical answer to the question of 'how to fight' was hard to grasp, or even believe a valid solution may be within reach. There was always hope, and that was all I could relay at the moment.

"Honey, you'll have to reach deep down and dedicate your energy to fulfilling life while fighting the effects of the cancer. Before I met you I had basically forgotten how to live, but now I know the parade won't just come through your living room. You've got to go out to the street to experience it, not wait for the parade to come to you."

"Do you still love me?"

"Of course I still love you." My hand clenched firmly in hers.

"I want to live." Her eyes glistened with fresh tears. "I want to go to the parade."

25. The Change

Following Sophia's operation in August, our lives changed instantaneously. Halloween gave way to Thanksgiving, and Christmas was approaching at a rapid pace, casting a surreal atmosphere on the holiday season. My life became concentrated on performing two tasks: going to work, and spending time with Sophia. Though students were still on summer break during her operation, she quit her teacher's assistant job shortly after the surgery. We tried one more weekend trip in September, a visit to the desert, but the excitement and motivation was gone in our drives, the shadow of cancer cast a wide emotional net that outweighed my resolve. After that, the excursions abruptly ceased; my ambition shifted from boundary expansion to comforting the life of someone I loved. The first two months after surgery Sophia would run some errands and get out when she felt well enough to do so. By the end of October, she stopped leaving the apartment altogether while most of her time was devoted to resting as her condition worsened. Sophia and I now found both of us, as a couple, grounded by a physical disease. One measurable in scale, defined features and outcome, as opposed to the nebulous fragments of mental ailments that prodded Sophia to get me out and travel in the first place.

Yet despite the grim physical realities, Sophia took her downcast frustration in pragmatic stride for as long as she could. There would be no miracle cures, no religious conversion, no fancy vitamin regimens, nor did she subscribe to exotic holistic remedies despite the overemphasized healing claims. Studying the hundreds of alternative options from around the world, Sophia remained realistic on living the life she was given, coupled with the advanced stage of her disease, as a more rational personal option over dwelling on far-fetched remedies. It wasn't a way of giving up, it was a calculation weighing the quality of an actualized life over unproven remedies, and I found that took more strength than anything over the endless searching. Strength beyond most people.

By December, my days took on a set pattern. A hospice volunteer would arrive at eight o'clock, I would go to work, and then Sophia's mom would come at about two o'clock in the afternoon and stay until I got home sometime before six. There was very little other external support I could rely on as I greeted Sophia's sobbing mom every weekday when I arrived home.

My mom would come over and visit when she was in town. My parents spent a few months a year at a small ranch in New Mexico. Evelyn was particularly helpful when she was in town—a natural caretaker as she had always been. A mother never fails to be a mother, no matter the age of her children. I had made my peace with my father after the abrupt call from the hospital the night of Sophia's surgery. Given the tragic situation at hand, they both commended me on wanting to take care of her.

I could talk with my parents in such a different way than I could with Sophia's family members. When I would see Sophia's mom, Barbara, crying in the evening when I arrived home, it was painful to witness. Neither of us could carry on much of a conversation. Barbara was very good at keeping food in the place and she cleaned the apartment repeatedly, a therapeutic task that served as a useful diversion from succumbing to sadness. I sympathized with Barbara's cleaning. I figured the compulsive ironing I used to engage in was just a way to quiet my overactive mind during times when just getting through the day itself had become a crushing burden. The way my pressed clothes looked didn't matter to me anymore as I became engrossed in Sophia's condition.

Outside of the apartment, no one wanted to hear the real story, the day-to-day struggle. People just needed a few quick facts and left the rest to their imaginations as to how, why, and the way in which I would handle the situation. Friends and acquaintances would walk away in mid-sentence with a pained look whenever I started to relate the gory details of the operation and the things that ran amok in Sophia's body.

I learned from this exercise that people, in general, didn't want to hear the deep story. Not because it disgusted them, but because they worried about being faced with the same scenario and not being able to handle it themselves.

The weekends became very long as no one from her family offered to stay with Sophia. By the time December arrived, she was scared for me to go anywhere except work. I wanted to be with her, but it was hard to sit the whole weekend without being able to leave. My apartment, once my agoraphobic safe zone, had now been replaced by the terminal condition of one of its occupants—and at times, under the heavy hand of guilt, I even wanted out.

As Christmas neared, I would ask Sophia repeatedly what gifts she wanted. I managed one day to bring home a perfectly shaped Christmas tree that brushed the top of our nine-foot ceiling. With great care, I filled the tree with ornaments and lights. I wanted it to be the nicest Christmas tree she ever had. Sophia loved the tree but didn't want any gifts, she just wanted to be with me. She would give lengthy explanations of her reasoning, yet my natural insecurities wouldn't let me fully accept that anyone would regard me as a gift, despite her declarations.

The thing I wanted most to bestow upon her was an achievement nobody could give. I wanted to give Sophia back her health. If I could reach into otherworldly powers to somehow deceive physics and reverse time, even if it meant dying for her, I would have done it. As I sat for hours with Sophia, I saw what little resemblance of her remained. Her condition deteriorated as cancer riddled her body with implausible speed. Sophia's emaciated face underscored her skeletal features and her skin had a yellowish tone; the cancer had spread to her liver.

Morphine became the cocktail of the day at the latter stages. Though Sophia had a strong anti-drug stance, she didn't resist the prescribed dosage when a hospice nurse brought over the first bottle. She would spend most of her time on our bed slipping in and out of consciousness, affected by the sixty-milligram Morphine doses. Her usual position was with her back propped against the bedroom wall, head tilted up, mouth agape, and lower jaw pushed back. Although sleep dominated her waning days, when she was awake, her eyes would shove upward in her head, leaving only the whites of her eyes exposed much of the time.

Many nights I would enter the bedroom and freeze in the doorway to see if she was still breathing. As I watched, my first pleading wish always was, *please don't die now. I'm not quite sure I can handle it.* The systematic response of what to do when she died went through my head. First: give her a kiss. Second: call the hospice nurse to arrange for the mortuary to retrieve her body. Third: call relatives and friends. I watched Sophia intently while mentally going through the list when her arm would jerk, an executed breath completed, and my feeling of dread subsided.

I wrote the three tasks down for consultation when the time arrived. The list became another piece of folded paper in my wallet amongst other lists, notes and currency that now meant nothing to me.

She would venture out of bed once in a while and walk around the apartment in a hunched-over fashion. Her eyes would roll into her head and almost close as she would forget why she got up in the first place. Her memory would lapse reading the clock, she would pause in confusion for a moment before determining if it was day or night.

I noticed how her chest muscle had deteriorated. Her breasts, once firm and round, were small and sagging, her ribs thoroughly exposed, as if she were a victim of a concentration camp. Her beautiful long, thick black hair fell limply over her bony shoulders and back. It had thinned considerably. The lower half of her body retained fluid and bile, causing severe bloating. The added girth contrasted her starving upper body. Sophia's once svelte physique now resembled an elongated pear. The organs in her body were sweating water and other waste but had no place to digest since her liver was barely functioning. The result was liquid settling into her lower extremities. The fluids filled up from her toes all the way to her stomach. Both her legs and feet were puffed to capacity. Squared off due to the excess swelling, her feet were almost club-like. Sophia at times expressed concern that her skin was going to split open and explode due to the excessive swelling.

I would watch her sway slowly about the apartment. The heartache left a thumping emptiness in my chest as I glanced at pictures of Sophia I mounted on the wall two months earlier, trying to remember the way she was as a healthy person. Her voice once strong, now slurred, her wit and intuition now a distant memory, her outer beauty now marred. It helped my sanity to look at those pictures and grasp what we had in our brief, interrupted relationship. Just shy of four months after the fateful surgery, it had come to this.

26. The Eve

When I arrived home from a shortened Christmas Eve workday, Sophia had moved from the bed to the leather sofa in the living room. Barbara was preparing homemade tamales for me as I greeted Sophia with a kiss on her forehead. Alexa was there also. I was surprised to see Alexa, she hadn't come over much in the past couple of months. Her absence wasn't from a lack of caring, she just couldn't seem to handle seeing her sister in such a degenerated state.

After eating five of Barbara's tamales, I prepared for a nap in the bedroom. My schedule since Thanksgiving included an hour nap when I got home to help me stay alert until one or two in the morning in case Sophia needed some assistance.

Barbara and Alexa kissed Sophia while she slept and left the apartment to allow me some quiet napping time. I drifted off within five minutes of flopping on the bed—stomach full of tamales.

I awoke from my hard sleep at seven in the evening, a three-hour escape, much longer than usual. As many families around the country were beginning to celebrate Christmas Eve, I felt alone, but remained thankful Sophia and I were together.

As I prepared to jump up out of bed, I noticed the apartment was completely dark except for the bluish ambient light emanating from the television in the living room. I took a few staggering steps to the light switch to check on Sophia.

She was somewhat awake, her eyes blinked when the ceiling light went on. I sat on the couch, nudged next to her body and gave her a kiss. The ends of her lips performed a slight upward curl.

There was a chemical smell around her and the back of my shorts got colder as the sensation of seeping liquid slowly flowed up the back of my upper legs. I lifted the white knit blanket wrapped around her body and noticed she was lying in a puddle of yellowish brown urine. As I pulled up her long undershirt, Sophia lifted her heavy hands and put them over her bare crotch, knowing that she had peed but couldn't get to the bathroom by herself.

"Baby, it's okay. Let me get you cleaned up. It's okay, don't worry. I still love you even though you went on the couch."

Sophia tried to smile but remained still as I lifted her hands above her head and removed her long t-shirt.

I went into the kitchen to get a roll of paper towels, and then to the small hall closet for some bath linen. I also brought a Morphine pill as an ephemeral attempt to relax her while I cleaned. It was a couple of hours shy of her next dosage, but I didn't want her to get too emotional or add any additional feelings of embarrassment.

"Here, take this." I slipped the small pill between her teeth and grabbed a glass of water sitting on the coffee table. I poured enough water to fill half her mouth. The bitter taste of the tiny pill made her eyelids clamp together as she swallowed.

"I'll get you all cleaned up," I said, as I dabbed her legs and the leather cushions with a clump of paper towels to soak up the liquid.

I needed to clean her backside, so I pulled a folding metal chair from the small patio outside and set it next to the couch and began lifting her. With her body strength almost entirely depleted, hoisting her up was like lifting an oversized box filled with a couple of complete sets of old encyclopedias. I grunted as I dragged Sophia a few feet across the floor and propped her in the chair.

Sophia rocked sideways to-and-fro on the folding chair as I wiped the sofa with a bath towel. With each sway of her body, she would rock down further until one large contortion toppled her to the floor. She whimpered a bit as her nude body settled limply on the carpet. I stopped wiping the sofa immediately and crouched next to her, getting my center of gravity as low as I could to prop her back up on the cold metal seat.

I continued frantically cleaning the couch with my right hand, while my left arm tried to steady Sophia on the chair. I finished wiping the couch as much as I could and then sat for a few minutes on the edge of the cushion. While seated, I continued jutting out my arm to secure her bending body on the chair. I contemplated how to lift her off the seat to clean the back of her body.

After the brief rest, I wrapped paper towels around my hands to transform them into makeshift cleaning mitts. I moved behind Sophia and secured my bundled hands under her armpits. I took in a breath and lifted her off the chair, using one foot to kick her legs far apart enough to help hold her weight. Her feet flopped around a couple of times before settling firmly on the floor about eight inches apart.

I got my weight under her, removed my left hand from her armpit, and started wiping her back. As I quickly swiped down her body, I noticed she had a large, urine soaked sterile pad taped across both cheeks of her rear. A hospice nurse put it there to relieve the bedsores that had now spread to consume almost her entire buttocks.

I continued wiping across the back of her body until my right arm, secured tightly under Sophia's armpit, started shaking from her weight. Not being able to hold her any longer, I set her down hard on the chair and caught my breath while keeping my arm on her neck to steady her body.

Deciding to try it one more time, I inhaled deeply and lifted her off the chair. I once again removed my left arm from under her armpit and wiped her back and thighs. As I lowered my left arm and rubbed in disorderly motions on the backs of her legs, I gave my right hand a hard twist in her armpit. *Crack.* Her shoulder bent back as her upper body weight propelled her forward, crimping her right shoulder almost all the way to her shoulder blade.

"Mistake. Mistake," Sophia garbled as loudly as she could and dropped to her knees as I could no longer support her weight.

The cracking sound made me woozy for a moment as I speculated either her collarbone was broken or her shoulder severely dislocated. Now seated on the floor, Sophia leaned against the chair with her head down and chin touching on her chest.

It was clear I couldn't continue cleaning her myself and remove the wet sterile pad from her—I needed help. My first choice would have been to call my mom and dad, but they were in New Mexico for Christmas. They canceled their trip earlier and were going to stay home because of Sophia, but I insisted they spend the holidays in New Mexico and not change their previously set plans. I didn't want to call anyone in Sophia's family; none of them would be able to stomach the situation. I didn't want to call out a hospice nurse on Christmas Eve, they had been quite helpful the past month and I felt they had already provided more than enough care.

The only person strong and reliable enough to help was Richard Haverport. I contemplated putting my best friend and boss in this situation, but had no other choice. I ran the three steps it took to get to the kitchen counter and retrieved my phone. With two quick hops, I returned to Sophia to hold her body vertical while I dialed.

When Richard answered the phone, he was at home with his two daughters and wife getting ready to open some presents. He agreed to assist without hesitation as I apologized for taking him away from his family.

Sophia remained seated on the floor leaning against the chair while I waited for Richard to arrive. As I placed clean towels over the leather couch cushions, I pondered how to prep him verbally before he entered the apartment.

It took Richard about ten minutes to arrive, thankfully it was not a busy night for traffic delays. His voice cracked loudly through the front gate intercom that announced his arrival. I punched in the access code so he could pull his truck into the parking area. I went outside to meet Richard, closing the front door and leaving Sophia to her depleted body strength. A few seconds later, Richard appeared on the winding sidewalk, walking with a quick step before stopping abruptly about six inches from me.

"Hey," Richard said, as he gave me an intense look, not knowing what to expect. I failed to give him details over the phone, but emphasized I needed assistance with Sophia.

"Hey Richard. Thanks for coming over. I know it's Christmas Eve and all, but I really need some help."

"No problem. Of course I'll help."

I moved back a step, almost shielding the front door. My eyes diverted down. I wasn't quite sure how to initiate the conversation.

"Uh… I hate to do this to you, but I need help lifting Sophia up and getting her back on the couch."

"That's it?" Richard asked, relieved at the task.

"Wait, it's not that simple. She's gone to the bathroom all over herself and I've got to clean her back while you hold her."

Richard's face sunk as he noticed the urine splotches on the front of my shirt and pants. The look left little doubt that he had figured out the wet stains were not just water.

"Now, before we go in, let's rehearse what we're going to do," I said. "First of all, I know you haven't seen her for about three months, so try to keep your reaction to a minimum. She looks nothing like she used to."

Richard nodded his understanding.

"Secondly, she's naked. I'm going to call you 'Nurse' instead of by your name, just in case she recognizes you. I'm not quite sure she will, but I don't want her to be embarrassed."

I walked behind Richard to illustrate the lifting motion I had tried earlier on Sophia. He stood silently as I sized up his six-foot, three-inch frame. He was taller and stronger than I was, so odds were he could keep Sophia upright long enough for me to clean her and remove the mushy sterile pad.

"This is what we are going to do," I continued. "She's sitting on the living room floor. I want you to get behind her and lift under her arms." I shoved my hands in Richard's armpits to demonstrate the procedure. "She's deadweight, so you are going to have to lift hard without stopping."

"Like this?" Richard turned around, faced me, and lifted my body an inch off the ground with his hands under my pits.

"Exactly. But, I want you to approach her from the back so she won't see you. Her backside is full of urine, so I would suggest keeping a gap between your body and her. It will also give me room to squeeze in between you two and wipe her off. There is a sterile pad taped to her butt that I'm going to have to remove."

Richard grimaced, formulating a clearer picture of the scene.

"I'll try to clean as fast as I can, but you're going to have to hold her using only your arm strength for as long as you can handle. You ready?" I asked.

"Shit, Wade. It's that bad?"

"I'm used to it, but it's pretty bad. If you have any problems holding her, just let me know. If you can't do this, it's all right. I'll understand."

"Okay, I'm ready," Richard said firmly, staring at the front door waiting to see what was behind it.

I was about to open the door when I paused and said, "Oh, one more thing… I think I may have just broken her right shoulder when I tried doing this alone. So try not to move it around much."

Richard's mouth gaped as his head shook in disbelief. I turned and immediately opened the door before any hesitation could settle into either of us. When we made our brisk entrance, Sophia was still on the floor with her upper body propped against the folding chair. Her long tangled hair fell over her slumped head, the ends of her black strands rested on the carpet.

"Okay Nurse," I said to Richard. "Get behind her and I'll move the chair." He positioned himself as his face turned bright red, then flushed immediately pale. Sophia lifted her head when she realized people were near.

"Honey, I've got a nurse here to help get you cleaned up and back on the couch." Sophia looked up at me and nodded, before recoiling in embarrassment.

"What nurse?" she mumbled.

"Just a nurse to help. It's okay, don't be upset."

She put her head back down and drew her legs in closer trying to conceal some of her naked body.

"Nurse, start lifting," I ordered. Richard hesitantly secured his arms under Sophia's armpits. As he raised her, I kicked the chair out of the way. Richard grimaced and exhaled a forceful grunt. "You have her?"

"Uh-huh," he moaned with his teeth showing, surprised by the weight.

I crouched down and wedged between their two bodies, frantically wiping Sophia's legs and thighs with a dampened towel. As my hand approached the wet sterile pad, I threw the towel aside and tugged on one end of the tape. It flopped off easily from the soggy wrinkled skin. I gave it a harder tug and noticed that thick layers of skin were peeling off along with the tape. It felt like I was pulling the skin off cold raw chicken.

I flinched as I pulled, not knowing if Sophia could feel the moist skin tearing off in thick layers. Sophia's body started shaking as I heard Richard groan in pain. He wouldn't be able to hold her much longer. I pursed my lips and swung my hand fast. The wet sterile pad tore off in one swift yank as the skin flaps that remained on her cheeks bent backward, resting against her body. It was a sight I hoped to never see again.

"Okay, can you put her on the couch?" I asked Richard.

He crabbed his way over to the towel-lined leather sofa and set her down. As Sophia fell on the couch, her eyes opened slightly. I skirted in front of Richard so she wouldn't see him.

"You can wash at the kitchen sink," I said, as we both stared vacantly at each other for a second, reflecting the distasteful task.

Richard walked to the sink, arms extended in front of him. He quickly removed his shirt and turned on the tap water to rinse his arms. I covered Sophia with a clean blanket and adjusted her pillow.

I went into the kitchen and watched Richard scrub his arms with controlled urgency. He wadded up his shirt, not wanting to wear it on the drive home. When he finished meticulously washing and drying his upper body, I scooted him to the door and escorted him outside.

"I didn't know it was this bad," Richard said. He panted as his shirtless body felt no cold in the chilly December marine air. "Why didn't you tell me?"

"How could I explain it to anybody? It's been like this for the past two weeks. It's getting worse… and fast."

"Do you want to take some time off work? Take all the time you need."

"Work is the only time for me to get away. The nights and weekends are becoming very hard to handle. If I didn't have work, I don't know if I could take this twenty-four hours a day."

"I don't believe this. That's the worst thing I've ever experienced."

"I know. Thank you for coming over." I wiped my hand on a dry section of my pants and patted Richard's bare shoulder. "Sorry I had to expose you to this. You were the only one I could call."

"No problem," Richard said, staring at the few cars passing by on Capital Avenue. "Do you need anything else?"

"Just get back to your family," I said.

I watched Richard speed-walk up the winding sidewalk to his truck. "Merry Christmas," I whispered as he disappeared around the corner.

27. Come to the Parade

A sudden bumping movement awoke me on New Year's Eve morning. In the darkened bedroom, I could make out Sophia's hunched-over profile sitting on my side of the bed. A large chrome flashlight sat tucked against her left thigh.

"I'm scared," she said. A static perplexed look washed over her face. "I have no function anymore. I can't think. It's time to die."

I stared at her profile while coming to a fully awake state.

Her slow slurred speech continued, "What would happen if you gave me all the Morphine? Should I do that? Would it make me go?"

"You will die soon." I grasped her left arm and sat up to give her a peck on the side of her forehead.

"But when?"

"Soon, Honey. Just go back to sleep and it will happen."

Sophia remained slumped on the bed as I noticed the sun had yet to flicker through the sides of the window shades. In a cautious manner, she freed the flashlight pressed snugly under her thigh and aimed it toward the clock mounted on the unlit bedroom wall. She adjusted the ray of light until its round beam settled on the face, enabling her to read the time. Eyes squinted tightly, she stared at the clock until the flashlight fell out of her hand and bounced to the floor. Time was still so important to her, although it really meant nothing. Her only responsibility was tracking her Morphine doses, the one sliver of control she had left in her life.

My head dizzied at the realization that Sophia wanted her life to cease. I always believed killing a terminally ill person pleading for mercy from their misery was something I could carry out. The actual situation, though, brought on a drastically different feeling. Sophia now faced acceptance of her mortality and was summoning me to assist in her death.

"You will be in heaven before long. Wouldn't you rather die with dignity instead of committing suicide?"

"Dignity? I can't even go to the bathroom without someone helping me." Her voice was delicately weak, yet it had an assertive tone. "There's no dignity left. I'm already dead."

Sophia no longer wanted to fight; she wanted peace. It would be best for her, and although I hated to admit it or even have the thought arise, it would also be best for me.

"When's my next Morphine dosage?"

"Two hours. Just rest and I'll wake you when it's time."

Her face wrinkled in clouded calculation. "Two hours?"

Sophia reclined next to me and stared at the ceiling. Weakened, her body could not sit upright for too long.

"Why won't you give me all the Morphine?"

"Because I'm scared, Honey. I don't know if I could handle killing you. I would have no idea how many pills to give you."

She turned her head slowly and glanced at the pill bottle on the nightstand next to the bed. "There's probably enough in there."

"Honey, you're the one who convinced me not to take my medication and I thank you for that dearly. But… now you want to die by some?"

Sophia gained the strength to smile. "That was different. You just needed some love. I'm dying."

I glanced at the nightstand where the large Morphine bottle sat and wondered if I could feed her enough to die peacefully. Sophia settled in closer to me.

"It's not that I'm trying to be sel ," I pleaded, "concerned with my feelings while you're in such agony. I just cannot bear to do this. Please, please, Sweetness, don't make me."

Her eyes rolled in her deeply indented sockets, not satisfied with my response.

It was unfair for a young life to end in such a tragic way, but the terrifying fear of not knowing how her body would react to an overdose made me hesitant to accommodate her last wish.

"Honey, it's okay to die," I continued. "It doesn't mean you were too weak to fight the cancer, or gave up. If you want to die, it'll happen in due time. Just let yourself go."

"Yes, I want to die," Sophia attested, before pausing for a minute in deep contemplation. "Remember the day after my operation when you told me about the parade and how I have to take charge of my life and shouldn't wait for the parade to come to me?"

"Yeah, kind of."

Her eyebrows lifted in a manner that looked painful. "What would that mean now?" Though dulled by disease, her mind was still able to reason.

"Well, if you wish to die, your body and mind will make that happen. They will, I guess, take you to the parade."

She turned her head and exposed a strained grin on her gaunt face. Despite her terrible condition, I was, as always, mesmerized by her fiercely penetrating eyes and innate beauty. I knew she could still negotiate with me.

"Wade, I want to go to the parade. Will you please take me?"

I drew my arms close to the side of my body while I felt an involuntary tensing in all my muscles.

"Wade," her voice trembled, "I said I want to go to the parade. Will you please take me?"

I pointed my head upward, felt a flash of torrid heat streak across my forehead and course all the way to the back of my cranium. My hands numbed while the tips of my fingers started tingling as if the appendages were falling asleep and regaining blood concurrently. A bead of sweat surfaced so fast on my temple, the drop immediately jutted its way out of a pore to forge a surrendering rivulet down my face. In that brief moment of mental overload coupled with acute bodily reactions, I accepted what I was about to do and prayed a higher power would also understand.

"Honey," I replied, exhaling a hard deep sigh of resignation, "I'll take you to the parade."

28. Swallow

It took me four hours to determine how to accommodate Sophia's last request in this world. I asked her repeatedly if she truly wanted to die. She held her ground stoically and avowed it was time to go.

I counted out thirty-five Morphine pills and carefully lined them up on the bed stand. I was procrastinating, recounting the little white circles of death situated in rows of five across and seven deep. There was no particular reason I arrived at thirty-five pills, it just seemed like enough to do the job—though there were over eighty left in the large plastic bottle.

Sophia remained supine on the bed with her eyes half-opened, almost relaxed, at peace with herself. I noticed her lucky red bandana hung loosely around her neck, which she must have affixed while I was pacing around the apartment in between assertions of finality. I stared once again at pictures of her displayed on the bedroom wall, attesting that all remaining pleasurable life was stripped from her.

I wiped a clammy hand across my forehead as I went into the kitchen and poured water into an oversized plastic cup. I took a couple of swigs, noticing how the apprehension made it hard to swallow the large gulps as the water creased my throat. Before returning to the bedroom, I closed my eyes thinking I was going to pray, but the only the words uttered were: *Time to do it*.

"Honey, you're going to have to sit up to take these."

Sophia's eyes widened as she pushed her weak arms down on the mattress to prop herself against the wall. Her right arm failed to bear any of her weight. I pulled under her armpits to help, noticing her swollen right shoulder from the mishap when I had tried to clean her the week before. The remaining cartilage around the area felt mushy to my conscientious touch.

"Put your arms down to your sides," I instructed, while carefully nudging both her arms next to her hips until she was almost sitting on her hands. "I'll put the pills in your mouth and feed you the water. That way, you had nothing to do with your death. I don't want you leaving this world by your own hand."

I flashed back to the morning in Arizona when I had a gun to my head, irrationally believing I should die. I couldn't even imagine at the time I would be in a similar situation, except now I was theoretically the gun. It was a horrible recollection, but I was thankful to be amongst the living. I felt fortunate to have fallen in love with Sophia, though I knew whether naturally or induced, she would die soon.

Her blank eyes followed me as I sat next to her. There was feeling beaming from them, but she didn't have the energy left to show it with any conviction. She pushed a deliberate breath out her nose as I rubbed my hand across her left cheek.

"Ready?"

"I love you," she said with no expression.

"I love you too," my shaking voice returned as I kissed her blistered lips.

"I'm ready," she said.

I methodically put one column of seven pills into my palm and lifted them to her already open mouth. After sliding the pills from my hand to her tongue, I grabbed the large plastic cup of water and tipped it toward her mouth. She labored to swallow as water flooded down her chin and soaked a corner of her faded red bandana before seeping slowly into her black t-shirt.

I repeated the process five times without a break until Sophia ingested all thirty-five pills. The activity, performed in total silence, seemed to happen in a matter of a second or two. The deed was done, no turning back now.

I removed her water-spotted shirt and carefully pulled the loosely tied bandana from around her neck. She grabbed my hand when I was about to leave the side of the bed to get her a clean shirt.

"Keep this with you," she said, grabbing the red bandana lightly. "You may need it."

I untied the knot in the back and straightened the fabric out. I folded it into a small square and stuffed the bandana in my left front pocket, the same pocket that used to hold my medication before Sophia ridded me of the habit.

"I'll keep your lucky bandana with me," I said.

I walked to the closet to get a gray sweatshirt of mine she liked to wear. When I came back to the bed, Sophia had resumed staring straight ahead.

"Lie down and go to sleep now," I told her as the clean sweatshirt dragged over her upper body. "I'll be right here with you when the parade arrives."

"Will it be a nice parade?" Sophia asked without blinking her eyes.

"It'll be the most beautiful parade in the world."

I snuggled next to her and wrapped my right arm around her stomach. She closed her eyes. I couldn't close mine—I was wide awake worrying about what was going to happen, how long it would take, and if there would be any complications. My fatigued mind raced as I waited for Sophia to step through to the inevitable.

29. Expiration

I remained by Sophia's side with my arm draped across her. Every breath she executed seemed to pound in me as if I were somehow connected to her physiology.

After ten minutes, I couldn't handle touching her any longer. I sat up on the side of the bed and curled in what resembled a seated fetal position. Wrapping my arms tightly around my stomach, I rocked my upper body in small, praying bobs.

Within fifteen minutes after taking the thirty-five Morphine pills, Sophia's irregular breathing labored even more. Wheezing and gurgling, there was a moist sound in her exhalations due to the liquid slowly creeping up her lungs as it no longer had any other place to go in her swollen lower body. I arose from the bed and began pacing around the apartment frenzied and scared, not knowing when Sophia was going to die. Busy tasks helped my body move, alleviating the perceived turmoil of what was happening in the next room. I combed my hair, washed my hands, and looked in the dryer to find a clump of unfolded clothes. My stomach drew inward as I contemplated pulling out the ironing board to tend to the dried clothes. I shrugged off the temptation and started methodically folding the clothes with my trembling hands, waiting for Sophia to expire. I wanted to be next to her as she drifted off to heaven, but I was so edgy, so wired and tired at the same time, I just couldn't sit for too long. There was no sign of the familiar panic, except for all the physical symptoms—shortness of breath, dizziness, detachment—but not the same racing self-absorbed thoughts as usual. It seemed to be justified, a whirl of intelligent panic. Sophia was dying, by my hand, and it had crossed the point of not being able to reverse what I had done.

After folding the clothes, I noticed the pile was out of kilter—shirts folded sloppily, towels uneven, and pants not creased in their correct places. Not a good job of folding, but the chore was merely an attempt to keep moving. And to my horror, only ten minutes had elapsed during the task.

I forced myself back into the bedroom. Sophia was in the same position on her back with her mouth agape. Her wheezing had transformed into a hissing sound, louder and more pronounced than before. I sat at the end of the bed with my back turned to her and rested my left hand by her feet. It took all my strength to remain there. I felt I needed to touch her, so I gripped my hand on her motionless right foot. Having some physical contact was important to me, but I couldn't bear to lie next to her and feel her body go through its last heaves.

I remained at the end of the bed, hand on her foot, turning around occasionally to study her face. The last look I gave her, she opened her left eye slightly. It was like she knew I was watching.

"There's music in my stomach," she gurgled in such a soft voice, I could barely make out the words.

Time seemed to stand still at that point as I turned away from Sophia and closed my eyes. My mind deafened as all things shut out of my perceptions. I felt sealed in an isolated box hurled into the blackest depths of the universe. There was nothing: no meaning, no physical structure, no time—nothingness. I heard her last words repeatedly play in my mind, engraining them forever into my subconscious. I never wanted to forget her voice.

Then, without any intense struggle or a dramatic hurling last guttural breath, the noise stopped—a prosaic cease of life. I sat with my eyes closed for a minute more before turning around. I focused on Sophia's chest area for a long time, waiting for some indication of another breath. There was no movement. My left hand released from her foot as I stepped to the side of the bed and placed my right index finger on her neck to check her pulse—*nothing*.

I covered Sophia's body to her shoulders with the bed sheet, situated her head on the pillow and closed her mouth to give her the appearance of sleeping comfortably. The task seemed to elapse in slow motion as I really didn't know how to feel or act. I recalled the list I compiled earlier and retrieved the folded and tattered piece of paper from my wallet as a guide.

1. Kiss Sophia
2. Call Hospice
3. Call Relatives

* * * *

Sophia's mom, her Aunt Beatrice, and Aunt Marlene arrived a half-hour after I called. It was a solemn gathering, all four of us just stared at Sophia's body, commenting on how peaceful she looked. They didn't know I had fed her an overdose of Morphine. Sophia and I would retain that secret.

Contrasting emotions swirled within as my exhausted body still seethed with adrenaline, even though I didn't need it anymore. Barbara, along with Sophia's two aunts, insisted I go and get some rest, perhaps at my parents' house, while they waited for the mortuary to take Sophia away. Even though my body needed a break, I didn't want to rest—nor could I if I tried. I did agree to get away, though I felt guilty about leaving. I had to accept that wherever I went, Sophia's body would be gone when I returned. As I gathered my keys and wallet, I told the ladies I wanted to spend a few moments alone with Sophia. I walked into the bedroom, closing the door gently behind me.

I approached Sophia's lifeless body, knelt beside the bed, and rested my elbows on the mattress. I clasped my hands together and dropped them gently until they were resting on her rib bones.

"Sophia, thank you for the life you breathed back into me," I whispered. "You are the reason I discovered love, happiness with another person, and the calm of togetherness. You asked little from me, but gave yourself fully. You taught me how to deal with my panic and resurrected the good feelings I extinguished long ago. I hope I gave you something positive in return during the limited time allowed us. You helped me more than you'll ever know. Thank you. I love you."

I kissed her on the lips, noticing her skin had already grown cold. *Our last kiss*. A strange feeling overcame me as I walked out of the bedroom. It was a sliver of peace combined with a powerful sensation of personal well-being. I didn't understand the reaction, but in an odd way, it felt stimulating. When I rejoined Barbara, Marlene and Beatrice in the living room, all three were looking at me, as if waiting in anticipation for a miraculous declaration, like Sophia had been resurrected and her cancer was eradicated.

"Thank you, all of you, for your help," I said.

Beatrice neared me, her magnified eyes beaming through her thick glasses. "You are an angel," she said. Her aging hand stroked my cheek.

"Angels have wings, and they can fly. I have neither."

The three women smiled courteously, though I could read the confusion on their faces from my statement.

"You get some rest now," Barbara said.

"Okay, I will. Thank you again."

It was hard to comprehend all that had occurred—Sophia, cancer, death. As I walked outside, I pondered for a moment where to go at two o'clock in the afternoon on New Year's Eve. I wasn't hungry, I wouldn't be able to fall asleep if I tried, and I didn't want to get drunk or alter my mind in any way. On the slow walk to my car, I noticed my perception of the landscape had changed. Colors were brighter, a few hibiscus plants I passed had the most vibrant red flowers I had ever seen. The wind ruffling the leaves on the trees was playing a melody that sounded like water tumbling down a rocky river. The air felt different against my skin. The shifting breeze pricked against the hair on my arms, creating a flowing sensitivity equivalent to being underwater. These perceptions, accentuated by fatigue, gave me no concern. I let the present moment lapse, out of my control. Above, I saw four crows flying, their long beaks pointing to the next landing spot against a cloudless sky. My mind adrift in shock and exhaustion, I imagined myself amongst those freely soaring birds, all of us windswept and searching out a landing place—a destination. That's what I needed, a destination. But there was no place to go. I looked back up at the airborne crows as they fluttered their wings to land on a distant rooftop. If they could find a destination, so could I. With all the stimuli adrift around me, an impulse popped into my head, one that was not greeted with the usual negative mental backtalk. I pulled my phone out of my back pocket, opened an app and clicked a few times to find what I needed. After the purchase was complete, I walked a couple of slow steps just outside the front door before hastening the pace to my car, determined to carry out my new mission.

30. Getting Air

I made it to Terminal 1 at Los Angeles International Airport after what seemed like a mile walk from a parking structure located in the middle of the expansive travel hub. I didn't dwell on any morbid thoughts during the ride to the airport. My mind let things flow in and out. I focused on Sophia and all the good things that came about from us being together. She was no longer here, but I tried to push the fact away as I drove. The one definitive decision was deciding on my destination. It would be San Diego via Festival Airways. San Diego for two reasons: it was a short flight, and I wanted to make good on the proposal Dr. Crouch brought forth eight months earlier in one of our sessions—only without a million dollars at stake.

LAX was bustling with travelers returning from holiday vacations, while others were heading off somewhere for New Year's. My senses were reacting much differently than the last time I was at the airport with Richard and Mundo. I wasn't terrified or obsessing about the impending flight. My body was floating through a dream on autopilot, leading me to the sky. As my ears registered the horns of impatient drivers echoing under the cement-framed concourse and the squeaks of wheels from people dragging their wobbly luggage, my mind was numb to the sights and sounds of the assemblage of controlled humanity. As I passed through the glass doors that led to the ticketing area, I failed to be concerned that Festival Airways had banned me for life from their flights after the botched trip to Las Vegas. When I purchased the ticket online outside my apartment, no alarms or blocks popped up on my phone when I input my name. I had replaced my old Arizona driver's license with one from California, so the license number on file with Festival was obsolete, and hopefully the license holder was a different person entirely from the one who took that fateful flight. With the exception of my name, the old information they had would be incorrect. Even if the airline kept lists like those of casinos tracking card counters, the challenge of sneaking on a flight from an airline I was banned from brought on the only twinge of anxiety—but I no longer cared enough to let that cerebral fireball cultivate within my body. I felt fortunate there was a seat available for the impromptu flight at such a short notice and as a bonus, the price was not overly inflated.

Though I had no carry-on, or checked luggage for that matter, I seemed to appear as just another traveler—a normal human, identical to the rest of the people I watched scuttling about the airport. I flashed back for just a moment about the fact that I had no medication with me—an old habit trying to make an ardent comeback. The lack of medicine didn't bother me and soon vanished from my mind. It was a peculiar sensation, one I hadn't been accustomed to for many years. I wasn't worried about being worried. But, like some old comedy routine, the worry about not being worried about worrying crept through my cerebral passages, trying to reinforce branded behavior. I imagined a gigantic foot crushing a bright sign that read in large letters, 'WORRY.' The imaging seemed to stamp out the sensation.

Though I had a digital boarding pass on my phone, for some reason I felt it necessary to confirm I was actually booked for the flight. I stood in line and stared blankly at the ticket counter, stepping ahead slowly until a very short male ticket agent greeted me.

"I have a confirmation for a flight to San Diego," I said flatly.

"San Diego… okay, swipe your license in the slot and press 'Enter' on the keyboard," he said.

"So, I'm confirmed?" I asked while a boarding pass shot out of the thin slot.

The agent tipped his head and looked at his screen. "Yes, the flight leaves at ten after five. Do you need to book a return flight?"

"No. I don't know when I'm returning."

"I understand. Any luggage to check?"

"None."

"Okay, you're ready to go then."

Apparently, Festival Airways had not retained a record of my banishment from the Las Vegas flight, at least from the information on my license.

"You're in seat 20 C. Your flight departs from gate seven and will start boarding in about forty-five minutes," he said. "Due to heightened security with tonight being New Year's, I suggest getting over there right now."

"Okay," I responded with a tight smile.

"Happy New Year."

"Right."

The security checkpoint went without incident as I was still expecting to be pulled aside, banished from the flight. After the full-body scan, about ten minutes remained before the plane started boarding, so I stood inconspicuously in an isolated corner of the terminal and watched people. I wondered if anyone was watching me, or if there were any travelers who could discern that someone I loved had just passed away, and I aided in her death. Or if any of them understood how momentous it was for me to be boarding a plane, or if they knew I had found love only for a few months before it was snatched away. The people in the terminal all seemed so unaffected by being cooped up in an aluminum tube for hours suspended above solid ground. Flying to them was as easy as jumping in their cars to pick up milk at the corner market. Their flights were to deliver them to a physical destination quickly and easily without pharmaceuticals or someone named Dr. Travel.

The flight to San Diego was solely to achieve a mountainous goal. Sophia gave me her life to get me to the airport—that was the simplified core reality. Yet despite all of society's pretensions to human exceptionalism—mind over matter and the innocent arrangement of cells before our beings enter the world—Sophia and I were ultimately a casualty of the random fraudulent nature of genes. Hers aligned to premature disease that took her life without recourse. Mine was manufactured through signals crossed in the intricate flash firings of the human mind. But no matter the outcome, I would have gladly stayed grounded the rest of my life to avoid losing her. Being at the airport was one of the many gifts Sophia gave me. Besides her love, her presence left me with the greatest accomplishment of all—a peaceful mind, life unbothered.

I mentally summarized the past ten months, from the break-up with Pamela to Sophia's death. I recalled with astonishment all the events that had occurred, like it was an out-of-body experience, a hyper-timeline delusion I was reliving. The memories whizzed by as I recounted them, but the sorrow of Sophia's death jabbed my body with oscillating pinpricks. I moved to the tall windows in the terminal and looked at the Boeing 737, the plane I was about to board. It was shining back at me without judgment or emotion—I was just another piece of human cargo going for a short flight.

"Festival Airways flight one-o-nine with destination to San Diego is now boarding at gate seven."

The announcement from the intercom created a subtle pang in my stomach, making my body squirm ever so slightly. I hesitated getting in line for a few minutes for no other reason than to conduct a personal assessment of how I felt. After the short deliberation, I determined that despite my predisposed trepidation, there was actually an eerie calm inside of me. My brain registered danger and attempted to prick my nerves, but there was not enough reaction to make me panic. Shrugging my shoulders, I got in line to board the plane.

I forced out a smile, handed my boarding pass to the woman at the gate and proceeded to creep through the brown double doors into the walkway. I kept my momentum going forward, getting sucked into the line of people passing through the cramped door of the plane before I could bolt back into the airport. I filed in, just as a normal person would.

My eyes rolled around the cabin as I shuffled down the aisle. Although I was exhausted and in a walking state of emotional concussion, I couldn't help but realize this was the clearest mental state I had ever experienced while on a commercial jet since I was a wondrous child. My inhalations brought in thick air, but I could breathe; panic didn't inhibit my respiratory system as it had countless times in the past.

I squeezed by an elderly man with a bulky carry-on and proceeded down the aisle. When I stopped in front of row twenty, I noticed a beautiful thirty-something woman sitting in the window seat. She beamed a perfect white courtesy smile directed at me. The instantaneous desire to curl up next to her and stroke her lengthy light brown hair consumed me as I settled into the aisle seat. I smiled back at her before turning my head forward and staring ahead at the upright tray table. I suddenly felt guilty. Then I felt sel … then depressed. Then to top it off, a panic attack rattled up my torso.

"Hi, I'm Donna," the woman said as she leaned her ample-breasted upper body over the empty middle seat.

I slowly turned my head, noticing her flawless teeth and naturally plump lips. My inherent desire and weakness for relief, which used to incite sexual anticipation, turned to aloofness while I stared at Donna for a moment as anxiety rattled my gut. My subconscious knew she was just being friendly, but I took it as a sensitive affront to my weakness.

"Look," I said, "you are gorgeous, and I would really like to talk to you, get to know you. I'd even like to get naked with you and kiss you from head to toe." I gulped some air into my lungs as the sentence was hard to complete. "But the only woman I ever loved died a few hours ago and I'm just too tired to even look at you."

Donna's smile vanished. Her luminous green eyes fired anger back my way. She withdrew her leaning body to her seat and looked out the airplane window.

Dizziness engulfed me as I prepared to jump out of my seat and run down the aisle. My body stiffened in bewildered apprehension as past troubles came rushing back within me. Like intentionally taking the legs away from the dancer, or muscle memory away from the athlete, learned ability was hard to reverse. Overturning a natural aptitude for something was even tougher. Now that Sophia was gone, I worried if my innate predisposal to panic would immediately fill the void of carcinogenic crisis and love lost.

As I was going to get up and escape the plane before the door closed, my left hand dropped off the aisle armrest and fell on top of a soft raised section of my pants pocket. The lump surprised me until I reached into my left pocket and felt a bundle of soft worn fabric in my hand. I clutched the fabric tightly, knowing that Sophia was still there to help me, comfort me, even after her passing.

I pulled Sophia's red bandana out of my pocket and studied it, unfolded it, and proceeded to wrap it around my eyes. I tied a knot in the back to secure it around my head. As the door closed and the plane started its taxi to the runway, I imagined passengers staring at the silent man wearing a tattered red bandana blindfold. I nudged my head deep into the seat back. A grin crept on my face. Unnatural aptitude had emerged.

About The Author

Charlie Elliott is the author of the novel Life Unbothered. He grew up in the South Bay area of Los Angeles and attended the University of Arizona where he received a Bachelor of Science in Business Administration with a degree in Marketing. As the founder of successful online business portals such as bison.com, Charlie is best known as an entrepreneur and businessperson, but his passion has always been writing.

Life Unbothered was twice named a Finalist in the 2007 and 2009 William Faulkner - William Wisdom Creative Writing Competition (2007 was under the title The Random Fraudulent Nature of Genes). In addition, an adapted passage converted to a short story received an Honorable Mention in the *Writer's Digest* Writing Competition.

Charlie resides in Lafayette, Louisiana and Idaho. Visit www.lifeunbothered.com or follow the book on Twitter @Life_Unbothered and Like on Facebook